Could she touch Mitch?

Suddenly Katherine was overwhelmed with
the desire to run her fingers lightly over
Mitch's bare chest as he lay sleeping in the
hospital bed. She recalled the thrill she'd
always gotten from even the slightest intimate
contact with him. Memories of their
lovemaking returned—memories so vivid
that she could almost feel his caresses, smell
the musky, male scent of his body, taste the
salty tang of his skin after lovemaking.

She wrenched her mind from those images,
reminding herself that making love was the
only thing they'd always got right. Their
bodies had communicated perfectly, giving
and taking exquisite pleasure with a wanton
energy that left them sated.

Their troubles began, she thought bitterly,
when they put on their clothes....

What happens when lovers *don't* live happily ever after? Author **Dana Lindsey** brought an estranged couple together for a reconciliation neither of them wanted—and waited for the fireworks! The result is *Second Thoughts*, her first Temptation novel. Exploring marital havoc is a venture into fantasy for happily married Dana, who lives in Dallas with her husband of thirty years.

Second Thoughts

DANA LINDSEY

Harlequin Books

TORONTO • NEW YORK • LONDON
AMSTERDAM • PARIS • SYDNEY • HAMBURG
STOCKHOLM • ATHENS • TOKYO • MILAN
MADRID • WARSAW • BUDAPEST • AUCKLAND

To Charlie,
who loves me and believes every word I write is a diamond;
and to Pamela W. Renner,
who taught me to distinguish between
diamond and cubic zirconia;
with many thanks to my critique group

Published June 1992

ISBN 0-373-25498-9

SECOND THOUGHTS

1

MITCH WOODS WAS HIT by a wave of heat as he exited from the arrivals area at Dallas's Love Field airport. Impatiently he looked around for a cab, and finally sighting one, he hailed it and got in. The cab's air conditioner whirred loudly, but blew only hot air. Wearily he sank back against the seat. God! The August heat must be getting to him. He'd barely been able to hoist his bags into the cab. Mitch shifted, trying to get more comfortable. Surprisingly, his whole body felt stiff. He could barely lift his legs—his feet felt like they were encased in cement. When he attempted to loosen his tie, his fingers were so stiff, it seemed to take forever.

Fortunately there'd be time to cool off and rest at the hotel. Then he'd look over the deal before calling Anderson. If his assistant's report was accurate, Kathie's company, The KD Line, was a good bet—short on cash, but long on potential. Kathie had done all right with her new company. Who'd have believed that she could start a children's furniture company and succeed? According to the report, Kathie had finally gained some business sense in the three years they'd been separated. But now, as before, she'd gone overboard. He sighed. She'd allocated too much of her operating budget to the development of a line of playground equipment. Consequently her company was strapped for capital. And that's where he came in.

When the cab stopped at the Adolphus Hotel, he pulled his billfold from his pocket. What the hell was wrong with his fingers? He fumbled with the bills, thrust them at the driver and muttered, "Just keep it," rather than deal with handling change.

Momentarily energized by the cool air in the hotel lobby, he followed the bellman to his room. Yet by the time he got there, his legs hardly supported him. Hoping that a short nap might rejuvenate him, he flopped down on the bed and fell asleep.

When he woke, the room was dark. He must have slept for hours. And when he tried to roll onto his side, his legs wouldn't cooperate. What the hell was wrong? Maybe he'd caught the flu. He certainly didn't have time to be sick. He had to complete this deal. Then he could take the vacation he'd promised himself for months.

Slowly maneuvering himself into a sitting position, he lifted the telephone receiver, dragged it to his ear, and called his doctor in Houston. When Jerry Miller answered, Mitch quickly described the weakness of his shoulder and leg muscles.

"Think back a few days, Mitch. Did you feel a burning sensation in the soles of your feet?"

"Yes, since this morning. Why?"

"That could be a symptom. Any breathing difficulties?"

"No."

"Any trouble swallowing?"

"No."

"Have you noticed anything about the taste of your food?"

"I skipped breakfast. Come to think of it, last night's dinner tasted odd." He searched for an apt description. "Metallic."

"Any bouts with flu or virus that I don't know about?"

"I had something three weeks ago. I felt lousy for a couple of days, but not bad enough to go to bed. Why the third degree, Jerry? I thought you'd say I've got virus *du jour* and need aspirin. Can't you just call in a prescription up here? The concierge will take care of it for me."

"It's not that simple, Mitch. I can't diagnose you by phone, but I'm concerned about your symptoms and their sudden onset. They may signal a serious illness, and you need to see an expert. Where are you?"

"I'm in Dallas. I'm bailing Kathie out again, buying into her company. Odd, isn't it, that she creates furniture for children, but she never wanted kids of her own?"

"That should be your last concern at the moment," Jerry said briskly. "Call an ambulance and go to Memorial Hospital. I'll contact a classmate of mine, Ed

Bryson, a neurologist. He'll meet you in Emergency or arrange for someone else to see you."

"I don't have time to be sick. I—"

"Call an ambulance, Mitch. Now. Talk to Bryson. Let's hope I'm overreacting, but don't take that chance." The line went dead.

Mitch wasn't about to roar into the emergency entrance with sirens wailing. Instead he'd take a cab. But when he tried to stand, his legs collapsed and he fell beside the bed. Struggling to his knees, he called the operator and asked for a bellman's assistance.

What the hell was wrong with him? He was in good condition, yet his body was weak. Drained. Cold sweat covered him. Rivulets ran down his back and chest.

MITCH SQUINTED AT THE overhead lights while he struggled to reconstruct what had happened to him. He must have passed out in the ambulance the hotel manager had summoned. He glanced up. He was lying on a bed, surrounded by four or five people who were prodding at his legs and arms with cold hands.

A nurse cut off his shirt. The doctor slapped small, goo-coated disks to his chest. He heard equipment humming, clicking and beeping.

His throat was dry, his tongue swollen and sluggish. He had trouble speaking. "What is it?"

"Just rest, Mr. Woods. Don't waste your strength."

Waste his strength with three words? Stubbornly, he repeated, "What is it?"

No one answered. Cold, paralyzing fear gnawed in his gut and he fought to control the panic sweeping through him. He searched for something—anything—that would take his mind off this nightmare.

The deal. He focused on Anderson's report. Lots of potential there. Yes, he'd help Kathie one last time. He'd give her a healthy company. That would be five times the amount she had a right to under the prenuptial agreement she'd signed more than six years ago. Then perhaps he could shed the traces of guilt that plagued him.

God, how he'd loved her. Then.

Happy Divorce, Kathie Woods.

ABSOLUTELY EXHAUSTED, Katharine Drake lifted her head and rubbed her neck with cramped fingers. Glare from the lamp reflected off the papers scattered over the desk, making her eyes burn. She massaged her temples with her fingertips and yawned.

Tonight she'd spent six hours in the bedroom she'd remodeled into an office, going over the figures the consultant had given her this afternoon. There was no doubt about it; she had to find an investor in a hurry if she was going to save The KD Line. Three years of her life, and her grandfather's, too, along with his life savings, had gone into designing, building, and marketing her furniture.

Katharine drew a deep breath and closed her eyes for a moment. No way—she wouldn't give up. She'd cut back on expenses as much as she could, but the furniture would be built; her employees would keep their jobs, and she would find a way out of her cash-flow crisis.

She needed someone who'd take a chance on a small company run by a twenty-eight-year-old woman who had no prior business experience. She remembered her ill-fated art-supply store. No prior *successful* business, she amended.

Perhaps she should take out an ad: Fool Wanted.

The phone rang and she rushed down the darkened hallway, hoping her grandfather was all right. Who else would call her at two in the morning?

"Kathie Woods, please."

"Who?"

"I'm a nurse at Memorial Hospital, ma'am. I'm trying to contact Kathie Woods. Mrs. Mitchell Woods."

"Mitch?"

"Are you Mrs. Woods?"

"I guess so." Of course, she was. Technically. "Yes," she added, feeling a little embarrassed.

"Mr. Woods has been admitted to Memorial. His condition hasn't been diagnosed, but he is quite ill. He asked that we call you."

Shock registered in her voice. "Me?"

"Yes, ma'am."

"He asked for me?"

The nurse's tone grew curt. "If you wish to see your husband, Mrs. Woods, he's in the intensive-care unit. He's fully conscious. Since there's no trauma—no injury or surgery—he can have visitors at any time. You should be aware that his condition is quite serious."

Katharine scribbled down the nurse's directions, then hung up the phone. Mitch was here in Dallas, in the hospital, and he'd asked for her. After three years of silence, he'd asked for her. He really must be sick.

HALF AN HOUR LATER, Katharine stood in the hall outside Memorial's ICU listening to Dr. Bryson, trying to understand what the short, balding man was telling her.

"Mr. Woods's arms and legs are partially paralyzed, and it appears that the paralysis is worsening. Something is interfering with the transmission of signals from his spinal cord to the muscles. Although I can't confirm it yet, I believe he has Guillain-Barré syndrome."

Mitch was paralyzed. *Dear God!*

She recalled so clearly the long, sinewy muscles of his arms and legs, his lean, wide chest—and the strength and pleasure she'd drawn from his embrace.

She'd repressed those memories for three years, but they returned as strong as ever. She and Mitch had been so good together . . . such a long time ago. When loving him had blinded her to their differences.

Katharine drew a shaky breath. She had to know all of the truth. "Is he in pain?"

"No, and he won't be. Nor is his body numb. He can feel pressure, pain, warmth, just as always."

"Is he dying?" she rasped.

"A significant number of GBS patients die, but the rate is declining. However, most GBS deaths result from respiratory failure when the chest muscles used in breathing become paralyzed. He's in the ICU so we can monitor his breathing. It's a positive sign that his respiration is normal at this point."

"Will he be . . ." Her lips refused to form the word *paralyzed*. "Will he recover?" *Say yes!*

"We can't predict that. It's far too early. We can't even confirm that he's got GBS until we rule out the other possibilities. Frankly, we won't know the extent of the paralysis until it stops getting worse. That could take days, perhaps weeks. Then we'll discuss rehabilitation. But you should be aware that there is no typical case of GBS. Some patients experience little paralysis, others are . . . more seriously affected. There *are* patients who recover one hundred percent, regardless of how ill they were, but most do have some degree of permanent paralysis, Mrs. Woods."

"Ms. Drake. Katharine Drake," she corrected in a daze, then wondered why her mind fastened on that pointless detail.

Mitch was paralyzed. Maybe dying. And he'd asked for her. Why? Since she'd left him three years ago, he hadn't contacted her. Perhaps, too, he had recognized their marriage wouldn't work. Her middle-class up-bringing had left her unequipped for a life as the "so-cialite" wife of a wealthy business executive. She'd never been comfortable submerging herself in that stultifying role.

But now Mitch was gravely ill. He'd asked for her, and she wouldn't let him down. If he needed her until Fran-cine and his friends arrived, then so be it. For a second she wondered whether he'd do the same for her, then suppressed the thought.

"Can I see him? Can he talk?"

"You may see him, Ms. Drake. He's alert, and so far, his speech hasn't been affected."

So far!

"For Mr. Woods's sake, I encourage you to be upbeat. Just be yourself. Don't treat him like an invalid. His re-covery is dependent on his emotional state as much as on his physical resilience."

Bryson opened the door to the ICU. "Stay as long as you like. I'll check on him tomorrow. Good night."

Katharine squinted at the array of medical equip-ment. The room was divided into two sections with three draped compartments on each side.

A nurse glanced up from a monitor. "Mrs. Woods?"

Katharine nodded, too stunned to correct the nurse.

"Your husband is our only patient tonight. We're monitoring his heart and lungs. This way, please." She led Katharine to the last cubicle and pulled back the faded yellow curtain. "Someone to see you, Mr. Woods."

Katharine steeled herself. She closed her eyes and sucked in a calming breath. *Be upbeat!* She opened her eyes, forced a smile and stepped through the opening.

"Mitch! What's a nice guy like you doing in a place like this?"

Mitch sat almost upright, his back resting against the elevated head of a bed that seemed too small for his six-foot-four-inch, broad-shouldered body. Even the white disks pasted to his upper body and the wires tangled in the mat of curly chest hair didn't detract from his muscular torso. She gazed at his firm jaw, his cheeks darkened with a day's beard. Her body tingled at the memory of the gentle abrasion of his hair-roughened skin against her face and breasts.

After all these years, and under the worst of circumstances, his strong sexual presence still made her weak-kneed. She grasped the bed's footboard for support.

"Kathie? What the hell—?" He moved his left arm slowly and grasped ineffectually at the sheet. He pulled it up awkwardly, trying to cover himself.

Katharine didn't know what to do. Help him? Encourage him to do it for himself? *Be yourself. Be upbeat.*

Miraculously, she found her voice. "What are you hiding, Mitch? Remember me? I've seen it all on numerous spectacular occasions."

"Why are you here? What do you want?" he snapped.

Katharine saw fear in his face. "Gracious as ever, aren't you, Mitch? I'm the angel of mercy you summoned in the middle of the night."

"Summoned? You? Why would I do that?" He tugged clumsily at the sheet again.

Katharine stepped around the bed and reached to help him.

His fingers tightened on the bunched fabric. "No!" He turned his head away from her. "Nurse! Fix this damn sheet, will you? It's cold in here."

Startled at his outburst, Katharine drew away. She waited silently as the nurse adjusted his bedding. When the nurse left, she resumed their conversation.

"Mitch, a nurse called my home and asked for Kathie Woods. It took me a minute to realize that was me. I have no idea how she got my phone number, since it's listed under Drake. She said you wanted to see me, so I came. Apparently there's been a misunderstanding."

She paused, then added coolly, "I had no intention of annoying you. Perhaps I'd better go."

Ask me to stay, Mitch! she pleaded silently. But why was it so important to her to be here, and why did she want him to ask her to stay?

"Don't go! Please," he added softly. "I don't remember giving them your name and number, but I guess I did—" His voice broke. "Thanks for coming."

"How can I refuse a request when you said 'please' and 'thank you' in one paragraph? Are you mellowing with age, Mitch?" Katharine teased, hoping to lighten the mood.

"Mellowing with boredom, perhaps. There's nothing to do in here." He regarded his immobile, sheet-covered body. "Except wait."

In the years they were together, Katharine had never seen Mitch frightened. His life was so controlled that his emotions rarely surfaced—except when they made love. Then Mitch had been beautifully, powerfully, explosively emotional.

She suppressed those memories. Instead she focused on the endless nights when Mitch had worked late, then come home and gone automatically to his study for several hours, leaving her alone. If he'd paid her a little more notice . . . No, she admitted to herself, Mitch's inattentiveness was far from being their only problem.

"If I'm your boredom antidote, I'd better get busy." She positioned the straight-backed chair beside his bed. "Do you want to talk about this Guillain-Barré stuff?"

"No. Please, not now. Talk about anything else you want to. Just distract me."

"Have you notified Francine?"

"No."

"How is my sister-in-law? I haven't heard from her since she quit writing to demand that I 'do my duty by you.'"

"She's between husbands again, so she has plenty of time to meddle in my life. She's searching for a replacement for you. You ought to see some of the candidates."

Heartened by his humorous tone, Katharine laughed. "Any of them probably fits the job description better than I did." He didn't deny it, so she continued, "Would you like for me to call her?"

"I guess so. But just tell her I'm in for tests."

"Why?"

"She'll wring her hands, but she can't help." He lifted a shoulder in an attempt to shrug. "The odor of rubbing alcohol makes her faint."

Katharine changed the subject, asking Mitch to update her on several mutual friends she hadn't seen since their separation. Neither of them mentioned their marriage. Nor their breakup.

When the nurse brought Mitch's breakfast and set it on the tray, he slowly grasped a large spoon and dipped it into the oatmeal. Katharine moved to help him.

"No, don't! Go get your own breakfast," he said brusquely. "You must be starved, Kathie."

Katharine found the cafeteria and bought and ate half of the tasteless scrambled eggs she'd selected before putting them aside. She looked down at her watch. It was eight-thirty. Her grandfather expected her at the plant.

Gus was her business partner and much more. When her parents retired early and moved to Florida several years ago, she and Gus had drawn together. They easily reestablished the closeness they'd shared when she was a child and they'd worked together in his shop designing and building furniture and handicrafts. She located a pay phone and called him.

"Keep the lid on today, Gus. I won't be in."

His voice was solicitous. "Are you sick, honey? You sound tired."

"I didn't sleep last night, but I'm okay. Mitch is in Memorial Hospital—"

"What's he doing in Dallas?"

"I don't know. They think he's got—" she enunciated the words carefully "—Guillain-Barré syndrome. He's paralyzed." Her voice cracked. "He could die."

"I'm sorry he's sick, but you owe him nothing, except maybe sympathy."

"I want to help him. I have to. I don't know why."

"You're still foolish about him, aren't you?"

"I didn't think so until I saw him again." She had trouble swallowing. "I hurt so much for so long. But I'm happy now. I like the life I've made for myself. I'm perfectly satisfied with our company."

"You've done fine, honey. You should be proud of what you've accomplished."

"Thanks, Gus. Right now I don't know what to do about Mitch. As you know, our marriage never really worked. He expected me to be an ornament to his life. I began to feel like some trophy he'd won and proudly displayed. What I really needed was a husband to encourage me to challenge myself. I needed a partner, not a keeper. It broke my heart to leave him, but I had to...or suffocate."

She fought back the sob. "But still, he's so sick, Gus, and he asked for me. I can't turn my back on him."

"Well, honey, don't worry about the plant for a few days. You know I'll keep that furniture coming out and get it shipped. Lord knows, you've put in enough time, especially lately."

"Time wasn't the problem," she said, half-defensively. "I spent too much money developing our playground equipment. Yet I still believe in it. The designs are innovative. But I've got to find an investor if we're going to start production and make payments on the loan. Our established products will carry us for a while, but not for long."

"That consultant fellow, Art Whosis. What did he suggest?"

"Art Harris? He told me what we already knew. We need cash within six months, or..." She stopped speaking when tears threatened again.

"You get some rest, honey. Try not to worry about us. We've made it this far, and we're survivors. I'll tell you not to worry about Mitch too much, either, but I know I'm wasting my breath. 'Bye now."

Katharine squared her shoulders, grateful for Gus's pep talk. He was right, of course. They'd find the money somehow. They had to.

She stopped in the rest room and splashed water on her face, then dug a brush and elastic band out of her tote bag and tied back her hair before returning to the ICU. She waited until a therapist finished testing Mitch's lung capacity and left. Then she reentered the brightly lit, curtained cubicle, knowing her question was visible on her face.

"I'm getting weaker, Kathie." His voice was matter-of-fact, but he was visibly disappointed . . . and afraid.

"Did Bryson tell you that?" she asked cautiously.

"I can feel it. I can hardly make a fist or move my arms."

Katharine's heart sank. *Be upbeat!* she reminded herself. "Dr. Bryson said that might be the case."

"I'm so tired. I can't stay awake for more than a little while." He shifted his gaze to the bed curtains. After a moment he closed his eyes, but his face remained tense.

"Then sleep, Mitch. You need to be as strong as possible to fight this thing." Her voice raw with emotion, she whispered, "I'll help you." *If you want me to*, she added silently.

Mitch's "Yes" was so indistinct that Katharine wasn't sure he'd really said it.

She sat beside his bed and watched him as he slept. He was freshly shaved and his hair had been combed. He'd suffered the indignity of being groomed by a nursing assistant, she realized sadly, because he lacked the strength and coordination to do those ordinary things for himself.

He slept fitfully, shifting his head from side to side; but his body—his perfect body—lay still. His rest was interrupted by one technician after another throughout the long day. Impersonal hands drew blood samples. Others helped him breathe into a tube to measure his respiratory capacity. Orderlies turned him from his back to his side. Two hours later, they reversed him.

Katharine watched Mitch's face each time someone touched him. Except for his clenched jaw, his expression remained impassive as attendants gradually stripped away his dignity. He stared at the ceiling in silence, ignoring her attempts to start a conversation. Finally he closed his eyes, and she wondered if he was asleep or simply shutting out the world.

THAT EVENING, DR. BRYSON reappeared. "How are you feeling, Mr. Woods?"

He studied the chart as Mitch muttered, "How the hell do I know, Doc? I feel lousy. Dammit, man, I can't move!"

"We're continuing to run tests, Mr. Woods," Bryson responded calmly. "Unfortunately, at this point we can only determine what you don't have. If the other possibilities are ruled out, that will leave us with GBS."

"There's nothing to be done? Just wait and see?" Katharine's voice grated in her own ears.

"And hope for the best. There is every reason to be optimistic at this time."

At this time, she thought. Bryson had a wonderful way of offering hope, then taking it away.

"I'll be back in the morning, Mr. Woods. Try to be patient. We'll know more in a few days."

Mitch cursed violently after Bryson left. His eyes filled with anger.

Katharine put her hand over Mitch's, surprised that his felt warm, strong, *normal.* "'Every reason to be optimistic,' Mitch."

Mitch withdrew his hand, slowly dragging it across his chest. "Give me two reasons, Kathie. Just two reasons to be optimistic."

"You're alive, Mitch."

"For how long? Didn't Bryson tell you people die of this . . . syndrome?"

Tears welled in her eyes, threatening to spill down her cheeks. "You won't die, Mitch." Her voice quavered.

"Wonderful. I'll live to be a vegetable. Look at me, Kathie. Really look at me. I can hardly move. People come in and turn me every two hours. I can barely feed myself. And it can get worse. So what's my future? Lying in some damn hospital for the rest of my life, communicating by blinking my eyes? Don't tell me about optimism!"

Katharine shut her eyes against his fury, reminding herself that she wasn't his target. But he couldn't yell at a condition. He couldn't yell at uncertainty. He *could* yell at her. After all, he'd had *years* of experience.

"Then fight it, Mitch," she shouted back. "You're no quitter. Fight."

"Against what, Kathie? How can I fight when I don't know what I'm up against?" His anger subsiding, he turned his face away and closed his eyes.

Katharine remained in her seat until Mitch's regular breathing signaled sleep. Then she tiptoed to the curtain, drew it aside, and left the hospital.

As she trudged across the darkened parking lot, she went over the events of the day—a single day that had brought Mitch Woods back into her life. Three years ago she'd fled, hurt and angry. She'd vowed never to ask for Mitch's help again. She'd built her company and she'd built her life. She'd matured, and liked who she'd become. It had been hard. She'd nearly faltered in the early months, but now she was strong and whole.

When at long last she didn't need or want Mitch in her life, he wanted and needed her in his. He'd never really needed her before—except in his bed. What did he want from her now? And for how long? Perhaps he only needed someone while he was sick and alone; and she was available.

She was too drained to consider what *she* wanted or needed, or what she could give to Mitch.

EVEN WITH HIS EYES CLOSED, Mitch could feel her presence, her vitality. He concentrated on breathing rhythmically, feigning sleep. He'd had enough of Kathie's pep talks. He still didn't know why she'd come last night. The nurse who called her must have laid on the guilt. He'd neither seen nor heard from her since she'd vanished from his life. Why had she stayed with him today, watching as he waited and weakened?

She needed money, obviously. Anderson's report told him how much. Maybe that was her scheme. She'd ask him for money after she'd charmed him, played the devoted—what? She wasn't really his wife anymore, and they were hardly friends. They had so little in common, they'd run out of things to talk about in an hour.

Whatever the reason, though, he was glad she had come. He'd needed human contact, warmth—someone who regarded him as a person, not a readout on a meter or a blip on a screen. Who else would have come? Who else could he have asked? Not Francine. Francine loved him, but she was incapable of providing emotional support to anyone. Not Sam Chandler. Mitch wouldn't let his vice president, or anyone else at Woods, Inc., see him like this. No one there should know he was physically vulnerable.

Kathie knew, and that had bothered him at first. He'd even sent her out of the room before he struggled to eat. But now it didn't matter. She was part of his past and, only momentarily, of his present. But she was no part of his future, so it didn't matter that she knew, he rationalized.

He wondered when she'd leave. He wondered if she'd come back. She had to. He needed her—her jokes, her teasing. Like it or not, he needed her damn pep talks.

He needed her beauty: coppery hair swirling around an oval face dominated by emerald eyes. Her skin was paler now, her freckles more prominent. Her high cheekbones had become more defined and she'd matured into an even lovelier woman. Her voice was richer, huskier than ever. And she was so small. Five-Foot Zip, he'd called her; a tiny package of sensual dynamite.

He felt his groin tighten and mocked himself. Oh, yes, he needed her. Practically on his deathbed, he wanted to make love to his estranged wife. Well, hell. At least something down there was still working.

But why had she come? What did she want or expect from him? He knew she desperately needed money to save her company. No doubt that was why she'd come. Ironic, wasn't it? He'd come to Dallas to give her money by buying part of her company. But the idea that she was softening him up for the same purpose galled him. Naturally she'd be tactful because they'd previously argued about money several times. He'd reluctantly cooperated—even investing in her art-supply store at a time when he'd needed every cent to expand his own business. He'd even philosophically shrugged off the loss of his investment when her store went belly-up.

Next, she'd decided to construct furniture, and had asked for another large investment. He'd refused, unwilling to further indulge her expensive whims. Within a week, she was gone. She'd written him a note and left. He'd thought she'd go broke and come home. He'd even envisioned the scene where he graciously took her back after she promised to change her ways. She'd changed, all right, he admitted. She'd become self-assured, confident. Independent.

Money had to be the reason for her attentiveness now. She hadn't wanted him in her life when he was well. She sure wouldn't want a dying man, or a cripple.

He heard the rasp of metal against metal, the curtain being pulled aside. He slit his eyes and watched her leave, her shoulders slumped.

As he relaxed and drifted into sleep, something about a contract flitted through his mind. He tried to remember what. But he couldn't recall any details and just drifted into sleep.

A male voice awakened him.

"Mr. Woods, it's time to turn you, sir." Mitch cooperated as best he could.

"What time is it?"

"Three-thirty, sir."

Day or night? he wondered. He had something to do, he remembered. He checked the orderly's name tag. "Eddie, when is your shift over?"

"At five, sir."

"Would you like to make fifty bucks for an hour's work?"

The husky man chuckled. "Sure would. Long as it's legal."

"First, bring me a phone. Then get the nurse to bring my wallet."

"Sure thing, Mr. Woods."

In a few minutes, Eddie brought a phone to Mitch's cubicle. He punched in the numbers Mitch gave him and held the receiver to Mitch's ear while Mitch explained that he was checking out of the hotel and was sending his "assistant" for his bags.

Then the orderly called a Houston number and Mitch said to his office answering machine, "Sam, I've changed my plans. I'm not going to do the Dallas deal. I'm extending my vacation a few days, instead. Tell Anderson. I'll call you."

The cryptic message would confound Sam, he knew, because Mitch never acted spontaneously. But Sam would have no idea where to find him for a while. He couldn't let anyone see him like this—weak, and damnably helpless. His company would go down the drain if people thought he was incapacitated.

When the nurse appeared with his wallet, Mitch instructed her to give Eddie seventy dollars. "That should cover cab fare, too. If there's any extra, keep it."

EDDIE RETURNED WITH the bags, and Mitch watched as he opened the briefcase and removed a fat envelope labeled The KD Line. Eddie tore the contents to confetti and deposited the scraps in a wastebasket.

"Good work, Eddie."

"I'll give your stuff to the nurse to put away, Mr. Woods. Let me know if I can run any other errands for you." He flashed a friendly grin. "The pay's sure right."

Satisfied that Kathie wouldn't find out why he'd come to Dallas, why her name was on his lips last night, Mitch shut his eyes and tried to sleep. But he could no longer restrain the terror. Lying on his side, his face half-buried in the pillow, he wept silently until sleep overcame him.

2

THE NEXT MORNING, Katharine stood outside Mitch's narrow cubicle and called out, "Ready for visitors, Mitch?"

His "Sure" sounded almost welcoming, so she pushed the curtain aside and paused in the opening of the now-familiar curtained room. The heart-monitoring equipment hummed softly and displayed endless green lines rising and falling in regular patterns.

His smile gave way to a frown. "Kathie, you look awful! What have you done to yourself?"

His mood seemed better today, she thought. His eyes sparkled with good humor as his finely drawn lips spread into a wry grin. Her fingers itched to trace the outlines of his full mouth. She suppressed that urge and instead responded to his question. "Still the silver-tongued flatterer, Mitch? You always could turn my head with flowery compliments." She glanced at her black pin-striped suit and plain oxford shirt. "This is my you'd-better-take-me-seriously-buster suit. I met with a supplier this morning. I've learned the hard way that businessmen treat me like a lightweight, like I'm fifteen and cute, if I don't dress the part."

"That explains the ugly black-rimmed glasses. They cover your whole face."

"Effective, huh?" She took them off. "Clear plastic. My eyesight is still perfect."

"Where's your hair?"

"I moussed it into submission." She turned slowly so that he could inspect the tight knot at her nape. "Pretty dowdy, isn't it?"

"No one will call you 'cutie,' Kathie."

"No one will call me 'Kathie,' either. It's Katharine."

"Kath-*a*-rine," he repeated softly, then added, "It suits you. You've grown up. You should have a grown-up name, Kath-a-rine."

"I'm so glad you finally noticed I'm an adult. I run a business, I run my life—quite comfortably, thank you— and I'm a responsible homeowner."

Mitch gave her a questioning look, and she continued. "You'd hate my house. It's big and rambling and ... umm ... needs lots of work. You'd call it ramshackle."

"It's not in Highland Park, is it?"

She laughed at the idea of affording property in Dallas's wealthiest enclave. "It's in Old East Dallas."

"That means half your neighbors have junked cars in their front yards and don't speak English, and the others are renovating yuppies, settling in the hot new neighborhood."

She groaned. "I knew you'd hate it, you bigot. You can't stand the idea of neighbors who aren't exactly like you."

"I didn't mean it like that. It simply doesn't seem like a safe place for you to live alone. I worry about you." His question sounded like an afterthought. "You do live alone, don't you?"

"I live alone, Mitch. But we've agreed that I'm a grown-up and can run my own life."

"Just be careful."

Surprised at his show of concern at where she chose to live, Katharine decided not to push the subject any further. "Did you sleep last night?"

Mitch nodded. "Did you?"

Thankful that makeup concealed most of the truth, Katharine lied. "Sure. Has Bryson been in?"

"He was here, but he didn't say much. He just studied my chart, asked a couple of questions, and said, 'Umm.'"

She settled into the hard chair beside Mitch's bed—and suddenly she was overwhelmed with a desire to touch him, run her fingers lightly over his bare chest. She recalled the thrill she'd always gotten from even the slightest intimate contact with him. Memories of their lovemaking returned—memories so vivid that she could almost feel Mitch's gentle caresses, smell the musky male scent of his body, taste the saltiness of his skin after lovemaking.

Determinedly she shut out those images, reminding herself that making love was the *only* thing they'd always got right. Their bodies had communicated perfectly, giving and taking exquisite pleasure with an energy that left them sated, temporarily.

Their troubles began when they put on their clothes, she reflected. Then she had to become Mrs. Mitchell Woods, up-and-coming socialite, consumed in an endless and boring round of social obligations and desperately yearning for a more fulfilling existence. Over the years, Mitch became remote—a man thoroughly dedicated to his business interests, and with little time for her.

She shrugged off her gloomy recollections. "Why are you in Dallas?"

"To look over a deal, a short-term investment."

"Were you staying at a hotel? If so, I can check you out and take your stuff to my place."

"That's been taken care of. I sent someone over last night."

"Should I call your office for you?"

"I've checked out of there, too. I'm officially on vacation."

"Good for you," Katharine responded.   "I called Francine, Mitch, and I told her the truth."

"Why?"

"She's your sister, and, in her own self-absorbed way, she cares about you. She had a right to know you're ill."

"How did she react?"

"After my brave stand, I'd like to say she was a tower of strength, but I don't think she really understood what I told her. If she did, she managed to control her alarm."

"She's not coming here, is she?" His eyes transmitted his dismay. "You know she makes me crazy."

"She will visit, but not today. She said she's got plans. She's hardly the typical overprotective older sister, is she?"

Mitch rolled his eyes, but remained silent.

"Were you and she ever close? Before your parents died?"

"No. Since she's six years older, we had little in common. When Mother and Dad died, I was a college freshman. Francine was supposed to control my inheritance until I graduated. When I pressed her about advancing more money a couple of times, she admitted disliking the responsibility and handed control of my life to me."

"I never knew that. So you put your nose to the grindstone and kept it there."

"I wish I had. In fact, I spent my college years indulging myself."

"It's hard to picture you as a spendthrift, a playboy. I've only seen the serious side of you."

"Only after I'd wasted most of my inheritance did I realize that I had to support myself and my family—" He glanced at Katharine, and continued. "I pulled together enough money to start Woods, Inc., and you know the rest."

"Bring me up to date, Mitch. What have you been doing for the last three years?"

"Working."

Katharine laughed. "I should have known that. No vacations to exotic places? No social life that isn't business-oriented? Still the same old Mr. Fun?"

"I really had scheduled vacation for next week," he insisted. "I was going to get a lot of rest." He scanned the tiny cubicle. "I had a more exotic place in mind."

"And a more exotic companion, I'd bet," she teased, not surprised that he chose to change the subject.

"Your life had to be more interesting than mine. Tell me about it."

"Looking for vicarious thrills? I'm sorry to disappoint you, but my life sounds distressingly like yours. I've been working."

"You might as well tell me about it."

Surprised at his flicker of interest, Katharine blurted, "I did what I said I'd do when I left Houston and came home to Dallas. I've taken college courses in business management. I'm nearly finished with my Masters of Business Administration, by the way. At any rate, Gus and I borrowed money and started building the children's furniture I designed."

She fixed him with a meaningful look. "The same designs you, as I recall, dismissed as 'utter foolishness.'"

"I never understood why you thought you could build furniture."

"You never tried. When I brought up the idea of furniture design, you stopped listening and started arguing. I never got a chance to show you my designs or even explain that I'd taken two college correspondence courses to learn a bit about the practical side of running a business." She drew a breath, pleased that she'd spoken calmly, without accusation or rancor.

Mitch's brows rose in surprise. "Come on! Give me another chance to listen."

Despite his mild tone, Katharine hesitated, bracing herself for his criticism, or worse, his dismissal of her accomplishments. "You remember my grandfather, Gus."

"Sure. How is the old guy?"

"As lively as ever. He sends you his regards."

"Like hell! He thinks I'm scum."

"My very perceptive grandfather was a cabinetmaker until he retired. When I was a kid, he taught me to work with wood. We didn't know it's impossible to start a furniture line with little money and no expertise, so we did it."

Recalling his relentless grilling over her art-supply store, and its dismal failure, she hoped he'd drop the matter. His adamant refusal to finance her furniture company had been the final blow to her hopes that she could develop her own interests, her own life, and remain committed to their faltering marriage.

"Are you happy now?" His gaze searched hers.

"I'm proud of myself. I'm not sure why having a career was so important, except that I needed to create something of my own, to be in charge of my work and of myself. Succeeding became even more important after I'd failed so miserably with the art-supply store. But I'd realized that my lack of business experience and skills made success impossible. I learned that the hard, painful way."

She paused and decided against recalling the details of that experience. Mitch surely remembered their arguments as clearly as she did. "Anyway, I've achieved my goal." She'd avoided his question. "I'm content, Mitch."

"Is your company doing okay?"

She smiled with far more confidence than she felt. Looking him straight in the eye, she said, "It's fine, Mitch. Just fine." Except that I'm drowning in red ink, she added silently, relieved that her smile never wavered despite his dubious expression.

WHEN DR. BRYSON pulled the curtain aside the next afternoon and announced, "I'm glad you're here, Ms. Drake, because it's best if the family understands the situation as well as the patient," Mitch's heart began pounding.

"Doctor, I'm really not—" Katharine began.

"Please stay," Mitch interrupted quietly. He knew his eyes pleaded with her. *If the news is bad, I don't want to hear it alone.*

"Yes, of course. I'll stay."

He watched a flush spread from her neck to her scalp and wondered why he was disappointed that she didn't want to be identified as his "family." After all, he was planning to divorce her. He'd waited for three years before admitting that she would never return. Since their marriage was over, they might as well lay it to rest. He'd often wondered why Katharine hadn't ended the marriage. Because Texas recognized no-fault divorces, he'd expected her to seek one, citing "irreconcilable differences." But then again, he bitterly supposed, if she hadn't lined up husband number two, she'd have no reason to divorce him.

In turn, the doctor regarded each of them. "As I mentioned to both of you, we've suspected that Mitch has Guillain-Barré syndrome, or GBS—a form of polyneuritis. Simply put, the nerve signals are impaired so that some of the muscles don't get the brain's instructions to move."

"A short circuit?" Mitch asked, surprised that he sounded so dispassionate. It was as though he were speaking of someone else's body.

"Yes. It's caused by a disturbance in the body's immune system. The body makes cells that destroy its own tissue. The most effective treatment is a drug that suppresses the immune system and halts the destructive process. Unfortunately, there's no simple test for GBS, so we watch what happens with the symptoms. We've tested the speed with which your nerves respond to stimulation, and the rate is decreasing. We've checked your spinal fluid regularly for increases in the protein level, which is the surest indication of GBS. The last test showed a marked rise, so now we're fairly certain that you've got it."

Katharine frowned. "What can we expect to happen, Doctor?"

Distracted, Mitch noticed she'd said "we" as if she planned to be around. He wondered if she would be, and for how long, if things got worse.

"I wish we could be certain, but there are no rules about the progress of GBS. Mitch, your decline may continue over the next days or weeks. Your condition may change very little, or it may deteriorate significantly."

Deteriorate significantly, Mitch thought. What a cold, bloodless term for paralysis—or death. Katharine put her hand in his palm. Grateful for her gesture, he tried to curl his fingers around hers as Bryson continued his horrifying monologue.

"That could mean loss of weight, loss of muscle tone. There's also a strong possibility that you'll have difficulties swallowing and breathing. It's encouraging that you haven't had those problems yet. Most patients have to use a ventilator for some period of time. Perhaps you'll be spared."

Mitch's mind latched on to one word. "'Encouraging?' I'd hate to hear you discourage a patient, Doc."

"I'm morally and legally obligated to tell you as much as I can about your prospects," Bryson responded calmly. "We don't know much about GBS because it's relatively rare, with only about three to four thousand cases each year. And there's hardly a typical case. Many patients do make a full recovery. One man was on a ventilator for weeks. His condition was grave. But within a year he completed a marathon—not at world-class speed—but he managed to run the twenty-six miles. I wish all outcomes were so positive, but most patients have some degree of permanent paralysis. As I've told you both, I can't predict the course this is going to take."

Mitch hoped his voice wouldn't reveal his panic. "I'm not sure I've absorbed all of this, Doc."

"I'll answer any questions, of course. And you should know that I'm optimistic about the outcome. With time and therapy, your chances are fairly good."

After Bryson left, Katharine asked gently, "Mitch? Are you taking this all right?" Her voice tremulous, she tightened her grip on his hand.

She looked so distraught he wanted to take her in his arms and comfort her. "Better than I expected. Maybe knowing what I've got helps." He faltered and paused to regain control. "They say fear of the unknown is worse than fear of the known. Go home, Kat. Get some rest."

He saw her struggling to control her emotions and smile reassuringly. "Trying to run me off, Mitch?"

"No. God, no. If I don't have you to talk to, I'll go crazy in this place." He paused, realizing his tone and expression betrayed his strong need for her. "You're worn-out, that's all."

KATHARINE SAT IN THE bentwood rocking chair that Gus had made for her fifteenth birthday. Too exhausted and restless to sleep, she rocked and rocked. Maybe Mitch would get better, but she had no idea how long he'd be in the ICU. Bryson had told them he might be hospitalized for weeks or even months. After that he'd go to a physical therapy center until he'd regained as much use of his body as he could.

His future amounted to a series of question marks. If they only knew to what degree Mitch would recover, they could deal with it.

Fighting back the tears that scalded her eyelids, she closed her eyes. Mitch needed her because she was convenient and no one else would commit so much time to him. None of his friends could leave Houston to stay with a sick man for an indefinite period. His sister was no help. So much for family and friends, the very people Mitch had always stood up for. That left her.

But she and Mitch weren't a team. They never had been. They'd lived together, but never shared their lives, never worked toward a common goal. He'd wanted a socialite who'd be a hostess to his business associates, throw posh parties, and help to raise funds for various philanthropies.

That had never been her style. She'd needed to be her own person. She couldn't live in the stifling environment that was Mitch's world, but she'd failed to make him understand that.

If they hadn't married so soon after they'd met, if she'd been more mature at twenty-two, more certain of what she sought from life, if they'd known each other better, there'd have been no wedding. Instead, they became a perfect example of the old adage—"Marry in haste, repent at leisure." She'd had plenty of time to repent, but she'd rebuilt her life in the process.

For the first time, though, Mitch needed her, and she'd responded to that need. What did she need from Mitch? Nothing. Not anymore.

Mitch had changed. He was openly grateful to her. While he was frustrated by his total dependence on others for every physical need, he bore the indignity with more patience than she'd have believed possible. He'd even treated her business with respect, rather than the condemnation she'd expected.

She was building false hopes! Mitch was very sick. Of course, he'd be grateful to the only person who'd spend time with him. He'd revert to his old, remote, workaholic self when he recovered. A tremor of fear coursed through her—*if* he recovered.

And what if he didn't? What if he never got better? She had to face that very real possibility. While Dr. Bryson had talked of optimism and marathons, he'd also admitted that Mitch's future was unpredictable.

She tried to picture Mitch as an invalid, his keen intellect trapped in an unresponsive body. Appalled at the contrast between that image and his formerly powerful physique, she tried to avoid thinking about that terrible possibility by distracting herself with her own difficulties.

Their marriage, such as it was, ended when she left Houston. She'd established the life she wanted, but still she hoped for the satisfaction and joy of loving a man who loved and respected her as she was. She admitted that Mitch would never be that man. But if he was permanently disabled, what would she owe him? How much of her time, of herself, would she give him? These questions preoccupied her, but she had no answers to any of them. She'd just have to wait and see. Katharine switched off the lamp and stared into the darkness. Perhaps the outlook for Mitch would be brighter tomorrow.

BUT TOMORROW AND THE DAYS that followed were no better. She stayed at Mitch's bedside from early morning until late at night as he continued to weaken. The muscles of his arms and shoulders slackened. His skin turned pallid despite his tan.

She didn't look much better, she acknowledged. The long days and evenings with Mitch and the even longer nights with the company's books were exhausting her.

Because it was impossible to distinguish night from day in the windowless ICU, Mitch had even more difficulty keeping track of the passing days. She wasn't surprised when he greeted her with, "What time is it? Hell, what day is it?"

She glanced at the clock high on the wall behind his bed. "It's ten o'clock in the morning, and it's Tuesday. This is the sixth day," she added, using a starting point she knew was meaningful to him. "How do you feel today?"

"Rotten. Every time I think it can't get worse, it does."

"Do you want to talk about it?"

"No. I've got no energy. I just want to sleep. I'm sorry you wasted a trip."

While he slept, Katharine sat beside his bed, reviewing her company's bills for the month. When an attendant brought Mitch his lunch, Katharine got up to leave.

"Will you be needing help with that, Mr. Woods?" the young woman asked.

"No." Mitch's tone dismissed her. Katharine watched as he tried to lift his fingers and grasp his fork, but his hand refused to cooperate. He clenched his jaw and tried harder, without result. Katharine's heart went out to him.

"Sh—!" He bit off the word and glared at Katharine. "I'm not hungry." His glower dared her to challenge him.

She settled herself on the edge of his bed. "No one is hungry for hospital food. But you have to eat in the interests of keeping your gorgeous body and rotten soul together for a while."

"Lovely word choice," he growled.

With careful nonchalance, Katharine picked up his fork and sampled the entree. "This is definitely pasta of some kind. Lots of lovely carbohydrates unaccompanied by flavor of any sort."

She speared a forkful and offered it to him. His piercing blue eyes filled with rage and resentment. His jaws were so tense that she feared his teeth would crack. Giving him her most winsome smile, she leaned forward and brushed the fork against his lips. "Come on, big guy, give it a shot."

His gaze locked with hers, Mitch slowly opened his mouth, accepted the food, chewed without enthusiasm, and swallowed. Coyly, Katharine lifted another forkful to his lips and favored him with an approving smile as he acquiesced. Pleased with her success, she sought to keep his attention away from his vulnerability.

"Remember when I fed you raspberry sauce?"

Mitch choked and she grinned as she held a straw to his lips for him to drink and clear his throat.

"No man could forget that."

Katharine smiled at the memory of the time they'd had dinner in bed one weekend at a hotel. . . .

She scooped up a little syrup on a spoon and offered Mitch a taste. Encouraged by his murmur of appreciation, she spread some on her lips, gave him a sultry pout, and invited him to sample. He licked it away—slowly, teasing her mouth with the tip of his tongue. Then she placed a dollop in the hollow at the base of her throat, and he trailed sticky kisses down her neck in search of it.

At that point Mitch took charge, and his fingers gently trailed syrup across her breasts, into her navel, and to other special places he thought needed flavoring. Taking his time, he then proceeded to lick and suck the sauce from her skin, arousing them both to the point of frenzy. . . .

Mitch's chuckle brought her back. "Cleaning up was fun," he said. "That was one hell of a shower."

Breathless, Katharine felt tremors of desire running through her. Suddenly she felt self-conscious about Mitch's intense scrutiny and about how aroused she felt by the press of his thigh against hers. To break the tension, she clambered down from the bed and stood beside him to finish the meal.

"You're chicken." The lazy sensuality of his inflection made the word erotic.

"You bet."

"Mitch?" A high-pitched trill penetrated the curtain. Mitch cringed and whispered, "It's Francine!" The curtain parted, revealing a tall, slender brunette, with her face carefully made-up, hair perfectly coiffed, and fingernails so brightly polished and long, it was obvious those hands performed no work.

"Mitch?" she repeated tentatively. "Do you know who I am? Can you hear me?"

"The whole hospital can hear you, Francine."

Clutching her designer handbag to her chest, she edged toward the bed.

"I'm not contagious, Francine."

"You look dreadful, Mitch."

"Thank you, Francine. You're always a comfort."

She lifted the shoulder that was closest to Katharine in minimal acknowledgement of her sister-in-law's presence. "Why is she here?"

"I asked her to come."

"You did? No. Of course, you're teasing me again."

Katharine didn't want to be part of this conversation. Francine had always condescended to her as someone socially inferior. Mitch would have to deal with his sister on his own today.

Suppressing a grin, Katharine said, "I'm sure you want to spend some 'quality' time together," and slipped through the curtain.

"MITCH, WHY HAVE YOU taken up with that woman again? Has this . . . syndrome thing made you crazy?"

"I'm feeling lousy, Francine. Don't start on me."

"I'm just so upset, Mitch. She called and told me you've got this strange sickness, and I rushed to Dallas. I never expected to find her *here*, though."

Mitch decided not to remind Francine that her three-hundred-mile rush trip from Houston to Dallas had taken five days. "Her name's Katharine, and she is my wife."

"Not really. Not since she deserted you."

"Don't be so melodramatic, sister dear. I was hardly Mr. Perfect."

"The years haven't been kind to Kathie," she crowed. "She's got those awful circles under her eyes!"

Mitch forced himself to be patient. "She's been here night and day for a week. I don't know how she does it. I don't know *why* she does it."

She patted the back of his hand. "But, dear, she needs money. You told me that."

Mitch groaned. "Yes, I told you that, and I told you that I'd buy part of her company, then divorce her. I did that in a moment of desperation when you nagged me again about 'tying up loose ends.' I've changed my mind."

He silently cursed his foolishness and swore he wouldn't give her the satisfaction of knowing he harbored the same suspicions about Katharine's motives.

"You know I tell you these painful truths because I love you, Mitch. I really do."

"Of course, Francine . . . Now, I'm really tired, and I can't get my breath. I'm . . . going to sleep."

FROM A PAY PHONE in the hospital lobby, Katharine called Gus and was gratified that things were going well. Her call to Art Harris was less encouraging. Although he assured her it was too soon to receive offers, he admitted that none of his contacts had expressed interest in investing in her company. The KD Line was still stalled.

Hoping to avoid more contact with Francine, she went to the hospital library. She read everything she could about Guillain-Barré syndrome with a growing sense of foreboding. Then she read about ventilators, and her fears compounded. The information Bryson had imparted merely skimmed the surface. Ten percent of GBS patients died. Nearly forty percent had significant permanent paralysis.

Fighting tears, she rose and slammed the book closed, the noise reverberating in the silent room. She clamped a hand over her mouth to contain her sobs and ran to the rest room. Locked in a stall, she sobbed for Mitch, for herself, for what they might have had, and for what lay ahead for him.

Fifteen minutes later, she managed to regain some control over her emotions, freshened her makeup, and returned to the ICU. When Katharine reentered the cubicle, Francine turned a stricken gaze on her.

"He said he was going to sleep," she whispered, "but I'm afraid he's in a coma!"

Apparently it hadn't occurred to Francine to call the nurse. It took all of Katharine's strength to smile reassuringly and ask loudly, "Mitch, are you in a coma?"

"No, I'm ignoring my sister."

Francine took Mitch's hint and left in a huff with a vague promise to visit again in a few weeks. As soon as the ICU door closed, Katharine said, "Poor Francine. Her brother's sick."

"My condition's...a great inconvenience." The warmth disappeared from his eyes. "I can't...catch my breath.... So much energy...to breathe...."

Her heart pounded furiously in her chest, and she slipped out of the cubicle to notify the nurse.

The hours dragged by as Mitch tried to sleep. Therapists came and went every half hour to check his breathing and draw blood samples. When the night nurse came on shift, she placed a thin plastic tube beneath Mitch's nose. "This is an oxygen cannula, Mr. Woods," she said, "to relieve your respiratory distress."

Throughout the night, Katharine sat beside Mitch's bed, watching him, waiting fearfully, her hand in his. The silence was disturbed when attendants brought a new patient into the ICU.

After things quieted in the next cubicle, Katharine opened the curtain a slit and recoiled. A large plastic tube stretched the patient's mouth and ran down into his throat. His chest rose and fell in time with the steady whoosh-thump of the ventilator at his bedside. Katharine stared in horror at Mitch's probable fate, then looked away. Near tears, she fumbled blindly for her chair and slumped into it.

"Ventilator." The word was a reedy rasp.

Startled, Katharine composed herself as she turned toward Mitch. "Yes. He had some kind of surgery, I think."

"Is it . . . awful?" His tone begged her to deny it.

She could not tell him the truth. "It's high-tech, that's for sure. You just lie back and let it breathe for you," she said dully.

For several hours they spoke very little. The whoosh-thump of the ventilator made it impossible to think about anything else. Mitch lay with his eyes closed, straining to breathe. Each time he opened his eyes, she whispered, "It won't happen to you, Mitch," and squeezed his hand.

Exhausted, Katharine finally lay her head on the edge of his bed, her hair spilling over Mitch's arm. Hypnotized by the relentless whoosh-thump, whoosh-thump, she fell asleep.

Drawn into semiconsciousness by a slight tug of fingers tangled in her hair, Katharine lifted her head and forced apart her sleep-swollen lids.

"Mitch?"

3

KATHARINE'S GROGGINESS vanished when she saw Mitch smiling weakly at her, his day-old beard a harsh contrast to his ashen skin. "I think I hit bottom.... Now I'm optimistic. What time is it?"

Katharine sagged against the back of her chair as tears of relief welled in her eyes. She glanced at the wall clock. "Seven-thirty. It's morning," she sniffled. She tried to blink back the tears, but they ran down her cheeks. She wiped at them with the backs of her hands, then searched for a tissue and blew her nose.

Mitch managed a thin chuckle. "Didn't mean to disappoint you. Were you hoping . . . I'd die?"

She was sniffling and laughing when Dr. Bryson arrived and got right to the point.

"You had a rough night, Mitch. For a while, I thought I'd have to hook you up to a ventilator. But by early morning your respiration was improving."

"Doc, have I . . . escaped the ventilator?" Mitch asked tensely, as if he was steeling himself for another blow.

"I can't make any promises at this point, but I'm quite optimistic. It's possible that you could lose more ground, but not likely. I know you want more precise answers, but there simply aren't any. In a few days we'll probably know more. Meanwhile I urge you both to take a positive attitude. If you remain stabilized for several days, Mitch, you won't need the constant scrutiny of the ICU. We'll move you into a regular room."

Katharine saw hope flicker in Mitch's eyes.

"You should expect to stay in the hospital for several weeks, perhaps months, depending on what type of home care you arrange. We'll begin a physical-therapy program while you're still in the hospital."

Relieved by Bryson's first truly encouraging words, Katharine realized she wanted nothing so much as a good cry, and the ICU wasn't the place for it. She got up and stretched, easing the knotted muscles in her shoulders and back. "Good news makes me hungry. I'm actually looking forward to breakfast in the hospital cafeteria." She wagged a teasing finger at Mitch. "Be good while I'm gone."

BRYSON FUMBLED WITH his stethoscope and cleared his throat. "Men usually want to know how GBS affects sexual performance."

Mitch clenched his teeth and muttered, "Yeah... I guess so."

"I'm afraid I can't make any promises about that, either, Mitch. But I'm optimistic about your chances for a full recovery of all your faculties."

Bryson departed with, "I'll be checking on you throughout the day. Get some rest. You've improved dramatically, but you're still very weak. We'll talk more about this later if you wish."

Good old Dr. Optimistic, Mitch thought. *What a roller coaster Bryson kept him on! First he raises hopes by delivering some good news—then backs off, promising nothing.*

Impotent. Damn!

For a moment, he longed for the warmth of Katharine's hand in his, for her smile, her reassurance. Hell, he couldn't talk to her about this. *It's not her problem*, he told himself grimly. *Not anymore.*

He couldn't confide in anyone. He'd cope with the wretched possibility alone.

THREE DAYS LATER, Bryson had decided Mitch was ready for a regular hospital room. When Katharine arrived there, Mitch grinned buoyantly.

"Look at this, Katharine—a room with all the features of a cheap motel: a hard bed, tacky drapes, and a television set with four channels. There's even a bathroom, which you may find convenient, even though it's of no use to me."

"Congratulations on your return to civilization."

"It's a morale booster. For the first time since I got here, I feel like there's hope of escape from this place."

"We need to celebrate. What would you like? I suppose the hospital would frown on champagne."

"I'll settle for a good meal."

Katharine consulted her watch. "Don't let them feed you dinner. I'll be back in a couple of hours."

She hurried to the supermarket, then to her huge, outdated kitchen. In three hours she returned to Mitch with a thermos and a picnic basket. On his tray she set out a damask place mat, two napkins, and a china plate, which she flanked with two settings of her silver. "The tray's not big enough for two plates, so we'll share one." She placed a single stem of miniature orchids in a crystal bud vase.

His look of anticipation warmed her as she dimmed the lights, then drew covered bowls from the hamper and filled the plate with artichoke salad, filet mignon, and asparagus with hollandaise sauce.

Recalling how aroused she'd felt at the contact of his thigh against hers the first time she'd fed him, Katharine decided that this time she'd stand beside the bed. She poured them each a glass of iced tea and inserted a straw in Mitch's glass, then cut several small pieces from the steak, picked up his fork and offered him a bite. She put down his fork and picked up her own to sample the meat.

He chewed for several moments and grunted appreciatively, "Perfect."

"I aimed for the exact shade of medium rare you like."

"You cooked this?" When she nodded, he added, "You shouldn't have gone to so much trouble. You could have gone to a deli."

"I thought your first meal as a semifree man should be more than a chicken salad and marinated vegetables. When you're up and around, I'll take you on a tour of Dallas's best restaurants."

She continued feeding them alternate bites. In a few minutes switching forks seemed too time-consuming, and she resorted to one fork. Sharing their food and utensils filled her with a pleasantly intimate sensation—one that she planned to savor.

It startled her to realize that she and Mitch had enjoyed so few companionable moments like this. She searched her memory and recalled a winter's evening when they'd sat together on the floor in front of the fireplace and shared childhood memories. But after half an hour Mitch had withdrawn to his study, and she'd stifled her protest. They really hadn't worked at developing intimacy, she realized. Yet tonight there was intimacy—and it had been achieved so effortlessly.

No, she warned herself. She wouldn't dredge up memories of the good times and start hoping they had a future. Falling for Mitch a second time would only hurt her again.

When they finished eating, he asked, "What's for dessert?"

Katharine hesitated, wondering about the wisdom of her choice, but quickly decided to serve it and damn the consequences. She made her tone teasingly light as she lifted the raspberry mousse from her basket. "Would you believe this is strawberry?"

Amusement glimmered in his eyes. "Not for a second."

She sighed and offered him a spoonful of the pink froth. He took the spoon into his mouth and closed his lips around the base. Their gazes locked and she saw stirrings of desire—and something else she couldn't quite identify—as she slowly pulled the spoon from between his lips. He swallowed, then licked his lips. She glanced away to scoop up another bite, then found him studying her intently as she lifted the spoon to his mouth.

His voice was soft and as silky as the mousse. "Aren't you going to have any, Katharine?"

"Not on your life," she said breathlessly.

"I hadn't realized raspberries were an aphrodisiac."

"I shouldn't have reminded you."

"I'd have remembered."

His intense gaze sent heat blazing through her. She dropped the spoon and stooped to look for it, grateful the tension had broken.

Why had she thought raspberries would be a cute joke? She'd forgotten that she'd have to feed him, stand so close to him, feel his eyes on her as they both relived that erotic memory. She grabbed the sticky spoon, then bumped her head on the tray bottom as she stood. Flustered, she scooped up the dishes and dumped them in the basket.

Mitch continued to study her with a quizzical expression. Unnerved, she focused on his left shoulder and said, "I've got to go. I have work to do. Good night, Mitch." She bolted from the room.

WHEN KATHARINE ARRIVED at the hospital the next day, she'd resolved again to restrain the sexual chemistry that ignited between them.

"I have a business to run, Katharine," Mitch said when she entered. "I can't let it go to the devil while I lie around wondering how I'll come out of this."

"Now you're talking! Work will be good for you."

"Let's begin with phone calls. I need to get in touch with Sam. Then I need to talk with several suppliers and customers. If you'll punch in the numbers and hold the receiver, I can get started."

Delighted with his take-charge attitude, so reminiscent of the old Mitch, Katharine called his office for him.

"Sam, this is your long-lost boss. I'm in a hospital in Dallas, but the worst is over." He explained briefly about GBS, then responded to Sam's questions. "No. Not right now. The timing is off."

He shot a glance at Katharine, and she had the odd feeling that he was talking about her. But that was silly.

Mitch's building-supplies company had nothing to do with her.

"I'm not ruling it out completely, but I don't want to go forward with that project right now. I'll give you the details later. Fill me in on our inventories. I figure I'm overdue on a call to Johnson at the lumber mill. We've got to be running low on pipe, as well. Hang on."

He caught Katharine's gaze. "Write this down, will you?"

She held the receiver to his ear with her left hand, and, using the tray as a desk, took notes with her right hand. He repeated a list of diameters of plastic pipe, then asked Sam about siding, electric wire and concrete as she dutifully took notes.

"I want you to send me the Dorfman contracts by overnight mail so I can review them. You'll have to do the head-to-head negotiation, Sam, and Dorfman's tough, but he's our most reliable source for composition shingles. I'll be available by phone in case he needs to be pounded."

Katharine smiled to herself. Mitch had lost none of the aggressiveness that had made him a success in the business world. His work was hardly glamorous, but he loved the give-and-take of buying building materials to sell through his chain of wholesale warehouses. He'd need that competitive spirit to beat his illness, and she wanted to encourage him.

"You need a speaker phone, Mitch. When I'm not here to hold the receiver, someone in the hospital staff can punch in the numbers and you can handle the calls in private."

"Great! I'll have much more freedom. I won't need you so much."

Surprised at the wave of disappointment that washed over her on realizing that Mitch wanted to be free of her, Katharine knew she'd been right—he needed her to help him when no one else was available. He apparently had no interest in reestablishing a relationship. Of course, she didn't want him in her life, either, she reminded herself.

"I have to go, Mitch. I have a business meeting, so I've got to don my real-businesswoman outfit."

KATHARINE STRODE INTO a small conference room at the investment firm, her confident smile as firmly in place as her glasses. She shook hands with the two men and nodded at Art Harris. Seating herself at the table, she handed each man a black folder labeled Three-Year Business Plan—The KD Line.

She drew a breath and exhaled slowly to calm her nerves. Opening her folder, she said, "Thank you for meeting with me today, gentlemen. I'll begin with a brief history of my company. Then I'll discuss my plans for a new direction—building the Habitat, a line of playground equipment—that will complement the children's furniture lines, yet diversify my products. Then

I'll go into the amount and type of investment I'm seeking."

She described her education, emphasizing the M.B.A. she'd nearly completed. She told them of her lifelong interest in furniture design.

One of the men interrupted. "Well and good, Ms., ah—" he flipped to the cover of the business plan "—Drake. Who runs this place?"

"I do, sir. Of course, I have a plant manager who oversees the production process. He's recognized as an exceptional craftsman." Gus would be pleased to know that he had an official title, she thought.

"I'm also the designer. If you'll look behind tab three in your folders, you'll find examples of my products." When neither of the men appeared interested in the furniture, she moved to the heart of the problem. "I should note that the furniture lines have shown a healthy profit for the last nine quarters. You'll find the financial history and three-year projections behind tab four."

The men glanced at the columns of numbers. One asked, "Explain the basis for assuming that you can be profitable in three years."

Feeling hopeful at this sign of interest, Katharine responded, "If you'll look at page twelve, you can see that I've considered such factors as increasing interest rates, costs of supplies, and payroll. Based on past sales, I think it's realistic to assume growth at approximately the same rate as on our established line."

When the men made no response, Katharine decided to move ahead with the presentation. "I'm looking for additional investment so that I can begin production of the playground equipment. I expect—"

"Thank you, Ms. Drake. I believe we've heard enough. We'll evaluate your business plan and stats, and contact you." The other man held the door open for her, silently commanding her to depart in haste.

Disappointed, Katharine packed her briefcase, straightened her back, and said politely, "Thank you for your time, gentlemen."

Alone in the elevator, she reviewed her presentation. Her plan was sound, and she'd presented it in a thoughtful, professional manner. But there was no hope that they would make an offer. Was it because they lacked faith in her abilities? Or was it because they believed that The KD Line wasn't a viable investment? It didn't matter which, she supposed, if their answer was going to be no.

She'd intended to visit Mitch again, but decided to wait until she was feeling more upbeat. Instead, she stopped by her house and changed from her business suit to a pair of shorts and a T-shirt. Then she picked up her sketchbook and watercolors, and headed for the Dallas Arboretum—sixty acres of colorful late-summer blossoms. For the first time in weeks she shelved her problems as she sat beside a garden and concentrated on sketching flowers.

Feeling refreshed, Katharine later returned to Memorial Hospital to face an angry Mitch.

"The Dorfman deal cratered," he snapped. "He wouldn't negotiate with anyone except me, even though Sam is more than competent." He ground out a curse. "How the hell can I run a business like this?"

"One lost deal won't destroy Woods, Inc., will it?"

"No. But I don't like to lose." He glowered at her and added, "Anything."

Did he mean her? *No*, she decided. His scowl was only a reflection of his general frustration. "There'll be other opportunities, Mitch. Soon enough, you can revert to your old workaholic ways and live for your deals."

"What if I can't? What if I'm crippled for life and can never get out of this goddamn bed?"

"Dr. Optimistic thinks you'll get better. Please try to be patient."

"Patient, hell!" he snarled. "That's easy for you to say. You're not trapped here watching your life slip away!"

Feeling her own patience wearing thin, Katharine gritted her teeth and reminded herself that Mitch was lashing out at his illness, not at her. "I read about GBS, Mitch. I know you've got a good chance of recovering. Lots of people do. But you have to want it. To work for it."

"Well, thank you, Dr. Woods! Or Dr. Drake, or whoever you are. I don't know why I'm paying Bryson when you work for free."

"Damn it, Mitch—"

"Or do you? What do you want from me? Why are you here all the time?"

"Because you're such charming company, and I have nothing better to do with my life!" Katharine struggled to control her temper. "I realize your life isn't a picnic right now, Mitch, and I've tried to be supportive. But I've had a rotten day, too, and I won't put up with your abuse."

She snatched her purse from the chair and stalked toward the door, preparing to fling a "Good night" over her shoulder.

"I may be impotent."

The blurted words stopped Katharine in her tracks. She whirled to face him. "What?"

He spoke in an unsteady rasp. "Bryson says it's possible. I wasn't going to tell anyone."

"How long have you known?" she asked, grateful that her voice sounded calm.

"A week maybe. I was still in the ICU."

Her heart sank. Mitch had coped with this devastating possibility alone for days. And she'd teased him with raspberry mousse, exchanged hot looks with him, then fled, ignoring the desire in his eyes.

Too late, she understood. Last night she'd seen hope and fear along with desire. Hope that he still attracted her. Fear that he could no longer respond. But as she'd pulled away, hope had vanished, leaving fear, and dismay, and regret.

He'd needed her in those moments, and she'd been unaware, occupied with her own conflict between desire and dread. Guilt swept through her and she shuddered. "Do you want to talk about it?" She cursed the quaver in her voice.

"There's not much to discuss. Just wait and see. Always, 'Wait and see.'"

"I know I sound like a broken record, but try to be patient. Your illness has stopped getting worse. That's a victory, isn't it?"

"That's a long way from recovery. And who knows how much I'll recover?" He muttered, "Impotent. Hell, I can hardly make myself say the word." He stared at the far wall.

After a few moments of silence, Katharine slumped into the chair. She, too, was at a loss for words. Mitch impotent? *Impossible*, she thought. But the mere prospect had to be devastating. Mitch had been a skilled lover who'd helped her discover the depths of her own sensuality. Perhaps he'd never again give or take sexual pleasure that once had been so easy for him to achieve.

Mitch broke the long silence. "Remember the night we first met, Katharine?" His bold stare dared her to deny it.

She remembered every second of that night. "At Tim and Janet's wedding reception. I'd just finished college, and I'd never been to a big society wedding. You were wearing your groomsman's tuxedo and looked like the Marlboro Man."

"I'd been watching you move through the crowd in that slinky, sexy green dress, yet somehow there was an air of innocence about you. You stopped under a chandelier and the light turned your hair fiery gold. Then you smiled at me. I was twenty-eight years old, and no woman had ever stopped me in my tracks before. But I stood and gawked at you like I was a horny adolescent. I'll always remember that smile and that dress."

Her throat tight with emotion, Katharine sat on the edge of the bed and slipped her hand into his. "You barely said two words to me. You just took my hand and led me to the dance floor."

"They were playing 'Some Enchanted Evening.'"

"You remember that?"

"Sure."

Without quite realizing what she was doing, she lay down beside Mitch and rested her head in the hollow where his chest merged with his shoulder. Katharine closed her eyes and let the memories flood her consciousness.

When the music had stopped, they were in a dark corner of the terrace. She'd looked up at him, her lips parted, inviting his kiss. But he'd teased her, made her wait while he slowly dropped gentle kisses across her forehead, on her eyelids and over her cheeks until she'd been desperate to have his mouth on hers.

Mitch chuckled softly. "And I'll always remember the way you kissed me."

When he'd whispered, "Stay with me tonight, sweetheart," she'd known she was lost. They were hardly inside his room when he'd slipped the shoulder straps down her arms and her dress slid to the floor. After he'd shed his clothes, they stared at each other for a charged moment before they explored each other intimately, with hands and lips and tongues.

Lost in her memories, Katharine stroked the smooth, solid muscles of Mitch's upper chest through the thin hospital gown. She felt the rapid beat of his heart beneath her palm.

"I loved touching you, Kat."

"I remember."

She vividly recalled their wild urgency that night as they'd sunk to the carpet. He'd stroked her until she trembled with pleasure, and whispered endearments as he thrust inside her.

"I had no idea you were a virgin until then. I heard you cry out, but it was too late."

"No. Not too late." He'd tried to withdraw, she remembered, but she'd tightened her legs around him and urged him on. In minutes, they'd reached the sweet agony of release.

"Oh, Kat," Mitch murmured. "We were incredible."

The light pressure of his lips against her cheek brought Katharine out of her reverie. "You were a superb lover, Mitch. You can be like that again. Give yourself time to get well."

Katharine sucked in a deep breath, sat up, and kissed him lightly, intending to climb off the bed. But when his lips parted and his tongue thrust into her mouth, a tiny moan escaped her throat and she succumbed to needs she'd been denying for three years.

She lay against his chest and slid one leg over his body. Her breasts swelled while her nipples grew taut and sensitized. Heat pulsed through her lower body. She felt his erection against her inner thigh.

"God, Kathie," he groaned. "I want you." His mouth took hers, cutting off her reply.

She wanted to be "Kathie" again, to make love with the wild abandon she'd known years ago. Dear God, she wanted him.

Yet, she was afraid of unleashing her passion for Mitch. Afraid of history repeating itself. Being with Mitch again like this was so tempting. But if she gave herself up to him, she'd also risk being hurt again.

"No," she whispered, responding to reason. She braced an arm against the mattress, slid off the bed and retreated.

Mitch stared at her, his expression incredulous. Even from six feet away she felt the pull of his sexuality.

"My God, Mitch!" She forced out the words in a harsh whisper. "I—"

"Afraid of making it with a cripple?"

Mitch's accusation tore at her heart. She owed him an honest answer, but didn't want to hurt him any more. She searched for the right words. "I know you're going through a lot, Mitch. I think I understand why you brought up old memories, why you want to have sex with me. The possibility of impotence has got to be haunting you. And it's perfectly clear that I still want you. But I can't."

She never wavered—even in the face of his anger— desperate to make him understand. "Making love with you was always exciting, Mitch."

Tears welled in her eyes, and she blinked them away. "I couldn't live with you. For a while I thought I couldn't live without you. I refuse to risk that misery again. So let's try to be friends."

"Friends? Hell, we're *married*. Married people have—"

"But we never had a *marriage*—not a real one. We made love, but it was only great *sex*, Mitch, that's all. We only shared our bodies with each other—not our thoughts or hopes or dreams. We lived separate lives under the same roof. We only cared deeply about each other in bed. We weren't in love, just in lust."

Tears spilled down her cheeks. "This time we'll be friends. Only friends."

4

MITCH GLOWERED at the door swinging shut behind Katharine. *Damn her!* What the hell was she trying to do to him? He wanted her with an urgency that shocked him. Tonight he'd felt the warmth of her body close to his, seen desire smolder in her eyes. But once she'd aroused him, she'd backed off, piously insisted on being friends. Because they'd been too good at sex!

He relaxed a little and grinned. Before she'd finished teasing him, he'd felt the pressure of an erection. He'd won that part of the battle.

But once he got it up, could he do anything with it? Could he ever make love to her again? *Hell.* He wanted to pound his fists against the mattress. But he was unable to make a fist or raise his arms.

As he replayed their kiss in his mind, he realized Katharine wanted him nearly as much as he wanted her. He knew she hadn't faked her own arousal, moaning her desire, plundering his mouth, pressing her body against his. He wondered if she'd spent hot, sleepless nights twisting restlessly, longing for him. He hoped those nights had been as frequent as the nights he'd wanted her.

He'd learned something else, too. Their breakup had hurt her. When he'd refused to back her furniture company, she'd moved out. He'd always believed that she'd done it unemotionally; because of money. Yet tonight she admitted there'd been a time when she thought she couldn't live without him. If he'd known she was as unhappy as he was, he'd have…what? Come to her? Asked her to come back? No. Probably not. His pride would never have permitted it three years ago.

Damn his pride! If he'd been willing to compromise, to admit his loneliness, to ask for a second chance, perhaps they'd have found a middle ground. But he'd left her alone, and now it was too late.

Katharine had gotten over him. She'd figured out what she wanted and gone after it. He admired her courage and determination, he admitted reluctantly. She'd become a mature, self-reliant woman with a satisfying life of her own. And she didn't want him in it. Though she did spend her free time with him, he couldn't imagine she was motivated by more than some misdirected sense of duty. She'd be better off spending the time beating the bushes for investors to save her company.

He closed his eyes for a moment, then opened them to stare at the ceiling. Katharine was right about one thing—they hadn't shared much of their lives when they were together. Building Woods, Inc., monopolized his time, leaving little for her. Some of the distance that developed between them was her fault, though. She'd been so restless, always dissatisfied with the pampered life he'd provided for her. And he'd given her plenty to be satisfied with.

If she wanted to have a platonic relationship, he'd go along with that for a while—at least until he found out what the future held for him; at least while he was stuck in this blasted hospital bed. He'd try it her way. But he'd find out what she was up to the next time he had a chance.

Meanwhile he needed to concentrate on regaining his strength and on his work. His business and investments might be all he had in the future, and he'd need all the strength he could muster.

Despite all the frustrations Katharine provoked, he could hardly wait to see her again. He stopped short. He'd assumed she would come back to see him. What if she didn't?

KATHARINE PUT HER PEN down and rubbed her eyes. She'd stayed up most of the night doing "no-brainer" company tasks, trying to stop thinking about Mitch, about the desire and longing he aroused in her, and about the things she'd told him.

She'd been stupid to get into bed with him, to let him stir up long-suppressed desires. But it wasn't entirely his fault that things had got out of hand. She was foolish to arouse and be aroused by a man who needed a woman— almost any woman—simply to see if his equipment still worked. After more than three years, it was ridiculous to assume Mitch wanted *her* in particular.

She stretched and went to the window. She shouldn't be so judgmental, she reminded herself. Of course, Mitch wanted sex. Any man faced with the prospect of impotence would. But she wished he hadn't tried to seduce her just now, when she was the only woman readily available.

She'd meant what she'd said about being his friend.

The instant flaring of desire for him alarmed her. She'd believed the past was behind her, but her response tonight proved that she was still far too susceptible to his sexuality.

And there lay the risk, she knew. In a few more weeks he'd leave the hospital and return home to Houston. Their lives no longer included each other. She wasn't his wife, and she wouldn't be his lover. That left friendship.

They had loved each other once, and she owed him something for that. She would be his friend and she'd help him get back to his work—his only real love.

Exhausted, she went to bed and slept restlessly.

KATHARINE SHOVED ASIDE the stack of orders cluttering her desk in her tiny office at the plant. Good old Mr. Broussard, her oldest and best customer, needed more inventory in a hurry. Ordinarily, she'd be gratified by the sale, but today she was out of sorts and dead tired.

The whine of electric saws and sanders amplified as she opened the door to the plant floor.

Gus joined her. "I'm getting the students started on stacking pieces for your big order, honey. Looks like business is picking up."

"I'm sure it will," she said. "How are the part-timers doing this year?"

"Good enough. The ones we trained last year are helping shape up the new ones."

Katharine watched a young man amble across the floor with no apparent destination. He'd only started working at The KD Line when the fall semester began, and he had an "attitude."

"Perhaps I need to talk to Cleve, Gus."

"Naw. He still thinks he's smarter than us working folk. Give him a few days, and if he's no better, Ernesto and Sharon can set him straight."

"You're probably right."

"Remember when you started this program last year, honey? Ernesto acted like a thug and rarely went to school. Sharon spent the first two months believing the whole plan was a trick."

"Nobody had given them responsibilities before or encouraged them in school. They're good employees now. We're getting our money's worth from them."

"Even with the bonuses you pay, based on their school grades?" Gus teased.

"It's costing a little more than I expected. Two of the kids are on the honor roll, and the other four are moving up. But the extra cost is worth it. Ernesto is thinking of going to college. So he'll be on the payroll for years." *If I have a payroll*, she thought, as her stomach knotted.

"We'll have plenty for them to do, and other kids, too, once we get started producing playground equipment."

"I need to make a phone call about the Habitat, Gus. Let's talk again at lunch."

She returned to her office and called Art Harris, praying for good news. Instead, Art told her the two firms that had expressed preliminary interest in her company decided not to invest. Sighing, she hung up the receiver. The Habitat wouldn't go into production yet.

She worked until nine, then decided to take papers home with her. For the first time since Mitch fell ill, she stayed away from the hospital that day, unwilling to face him, feeling depressed about her business and in such turmoil over him.

KATHARINE STOOD BY the hospital-room door and watched Mitch the next morning. All his attention was focused on the hand grip he was squeezing. He stared at his fingers as if willing them to tighten their hold.

As she watched him struggle, Katharine noticed changes in him. The pallor he'd developed in the ICU was gone. He seemed stronger, more in command, even though she knew his arms and hands were still weak and his legs almost totally paralyzed.

"That's fine, Mr. Woods," the therapist said encouragingly. Mitch relaxed his grip and let his head fall back against the pillow, sweat beading his forehead.

"You're gaining strength in the left hand, too, sir. That's very good. We'll try again this afternoon," he said as he lifted each of Mitch's arms into a large sling suspended from horizontal poles above the bed. "These contraptions will support your arms and allow more use of your hands."

As the young man prepared to leave, Katharine came in and said cheerfully, "Better and better, Mitch. Way to go!"

"Well, well, it's my personal cheerleader," he growled, a humorous glint in his eyes. He nodded at the large package she carried. "Did you bring me a present?"

She put the package beside him. "I have something to help set you free—the ideal equipment for the temporarily handicapped executive." She unwrapped the gift. "Ta-da! It's a big-button phone!"

Mitch gave her a quizzical look.

Katharine plugged it in. "Using this with your speaker phone, you can call anyone in the world on your own."

With the sling supporting his arm, Mitch awkwardly extended a hand to press the large buttons. He grinned as each one responded easily to the slightest pressure of his finger. "I've got to try this out." He dialed his office.

"Sam? I just got a great gift from my—from Katharine." He described the phone, then got down to business.

Mitch immersed himself in his work, automatically reverting to his old habits. As usual, he had no time for her. Not even time to thank her for his new phone. Feeling disappointed and rejected, she headed for the door.

"Wait, Katharine. I'm nearly finished with this call, and we need to talk."

Did Mitch want to talk about what had happened two nights ago? She wasn't sure she could handle going over that incident in the cold light of day. Sitting down, she marshaled her courage while he finished his conversation.

"Overnight mail is too slow. Can you get a fax machine set up in here?" Mitch asked.

Taken aback by his unexpected request, she snapped, "You're the man with a big-button phone and newfound independence. You make the calls."

He fixed her with a look of mock condescension. "I'm also a busy executive. I don't have time to make calls like that. It seems I'm going to need a part-time secretary."

"Don't you have one full-time in Houston?"

"Sure. But I need help here, too." He eyed her speculatively. "How's your typing?" he teased.

"Wretched. Besides, I have a business to run. Why don't you contact a temporary service?"

Uncomfortable with the tension between them, Katharine fidgeted. She'd anticipated a confrontation, or even a joke, but Mitch had the gall to treat her as if she were his clerical assistant.

"Okay. I'll get the numbers from Directory Assistance sometime. Were you working on something big yesterday? Is that why you didn't come to see me?"

Startled by Mitch's virtual admission that he'd missed her, Katharine responded. "No. I just had a lot to do."

"I take up too much of your time, don't I?"

What did he expect of her? His expression was bland, as though the question were casual. But she chose her words carefully.

"No. Except for the first night, you've never asked me to be here."

"Because you always were here when I needed you." Tension lines deepened around his eyes and mouth. "But now I'm getting better, and I don't need you around so much. You ought to spend more time with your company."

"I wish I had a tape recorder! I never thought I'd hear those words from your lips!"

"I remember how tough it was when I started Woods, Inc. I worked night and day for years. Instead of entertaining me, you should be at work."

He paused for a moment, then continued. "Tell me more about your company."

"I design and we build furniture for kids' rooms—beds, dressers, chairs, toy boxes, wooden horses. We just started selling a new bed for young girls. It's shaped like a swan. I suspect that grandmothers buy lots of my pieces, especially the old-fashioned ones."

"Who's your market?"

"Yuppies. My products are available at exclusive shops. I advertise custom-designed pieces in *Town and Country, Ultra,* and *Architectural Digest.* For the past year I've been working on something besides furniture. I've designed five pieces of playground equipment, the Habitat. Each piece is made of a special kind of plastic pipe."

"I hate to break this to you, Kat, but there's lots of plastic stuff out there. I don't know much about kids, but even I know that."

"But mine is stronger, longer-lasting, and safer." She threw her shoulders back and added with pride, "And more fun!"

"So when can I expect to see this stuff in my neighbors' yards?"

Katharine felt her bravado slip. She should have known he'd ask the logical question: When? "I'm not sure. Finding the right plastic pipe was costly. I needed a special combination of strength and flexibility that wasn't on the market. I had to pay the development and testing costs. I went over budget, but I have a strong, safe product that kids will adore and that can be built so inexpensively that schools can afford it. But I have a temporary cash-flow problem. When I recover those extra expenses, I'll start production."

Wanting to avoid further discussion of her finances, Katharine asked, "Have I told you about the high school students who work part-time at the plant?"

As KATHARINE RATTLED ON about her "kids," Mitch considered ways he could have helped The KD Line. Hell, he stocked dozens of kinds of plastic pipe. How easily he could have helped with development and testing. If he'd known . . . But she hadn't wanted him to know. Remembering how he'd let her down before, he certainly couldn't blame her for not asking.

"I could lend you the money. How much do you need?" he asked nonchalantly.

"Is this a joke? *You* lend *me* money? Voluntarily?" Katharine teased.

"I can afford it."

"You always could, but you refused to help me start my company." She spoke matter-of-factly, but he heard the resentment in her voice.

"Come on. Be fair. After all, my investment in your art-supply store had been a total write-off six months earlier," he said, disliking how defensive he sounded.

"I needed more than money, then. I needed business guidance after I got in over my head, but you weren't available."

"I was working sixteen hours a day. I didn't have time for you." Shocked at his own admission, Mitch cringed. For years he'd blamed her for her dissatisfaction with their lives. He'd given her everything, except what she'd needed—his time, his caring.

He cleared his throat and returned to his business plan. "Well, since you've developed skills, you don't need my advice. But I'll help you out with a long-term, no interest loan. To be paid back whenever you can. No strings attached."

Mitch had just intended to test her out because he still didn't fully trust her. Why had he been so unexpectedly generous? Because it would take her several years to pay off a big loan, and if she accepted his money, he'd see her from time to time—even if it was only business.

"That's very kind, Mitch, but I can't ask you for money."

"That's what *friends* are for. And, you didn't ask. I volunteered."

"I don't want to rely on you again. I like being independent. But thanks for the offer, friend."

She sounded gracious, but determined. "Do you really think we can be just friends, Katharine?"

Her expression was wary as she responded, "I don't know, but I'd like to try. I do believe it's the only relationship we could have."

THE PHONE RANG. *Damn!* Katharine was annoyed at being interrupted from her work at home that night by yet another phone call. She hurried down the hall and lifted the receiver.

"It's the man with the big-button phone."

She held her breath, fearing something was wrong.

"After you left, I realized I'd forgotten to thank you for your gift and for helping me become more independent."

A warm glow spread through Katharine. "You're welcome, Mitch."

"You never used to support my need to work, you know." His tone was free of criticism.

"No. I used to resent it because work was all you cared about," she said, surprised at how easily she'd admitted a truth she'd long held secret. "Everything's changed now, of course. Right now, I think working is therapeutic for you."

His tone suddenly changed, becoming gruff, as if he was struggling to maintain his control. "Yes, it's good therapy. Good night, Katharine."

Before she could respond, she heard the click of his receiver. *Damn him!* Just when she thought she'd figured him out, he did something totally unexpected.

SINCE MITCH HAD encouraged her to spend less time with him, over the next two weeks Katharine stopped at the hospital every other evening after work. She always sat at a safe distance from Mitch and temptation. They talked about business matters, the *Wall Street Journal*'s latest crusade—everything but their feelings.

Sometimes she even had to fight the urge to leave work and spend time with him. At night, he filled her dreams more often than not, until she would awaken, hot and restless and filled with longing.

As Katharine prepared to leave the hospital one Saturday, Dr. Bryson appeared. "I've got good news for you, Mitch. In another week I expect we'll be finished with your treatment. You'll be ready to leave us."

Katharine heaved a long sigh of relief.

Mitch surveyed his still-nearly-paralyzed body. "I guess I won't be walking out of here, Doc," he quipped. "Where will I go?"

"You have a few choices. Many patients with your degree of paralysis select an in-patient rehabilitation center. You should expect to stay several months, probably longer. But some patients choose to live at home and travel to the rehab center daily. That means using a specially equipped van and having nurses on duty at home."

"I'll have to think about it, Doc. At the moment, I'm so pleased about escaping this place that I just want to lie here and grin for a while."

"Fair enough. I'll bring you a list of recommended facilities in the Houston area and you can start making arrangements." With that, Bryson left.

Mitch's eyes gleamed with excitement. "Hallelujah!" he shouted. "I'm nearly a free man! I'm going home!"

"This calls for a celebration, Mitch."

He laughed—the happiest sound she'd heard in a long time. "I don't think we can go dancing."

"No, but I've got an idea." She headed for the door. "Don't check out while I'm gone," she warned.

Katharine resolved to avoid repeating the mistakes of their last celebration. Gourmet dinners presented too many opportunities for intimate touching.

In an hour she reappeared with her VCR, two movies, and the picnic hamper. "I thought you'd like a reminder of the outside world. Pretend we're in a tiny theater." She unpacked a tub of popcorn, a box of chocolate-covered mints, and a large cup of watery cola.

Mitch's face lit up. "I see you've brought all the necessities."

She fed him several pieces of popcorn, her fingertips brushing his smooth lips and the rough stubble on his cheeks. She drew her hand back quickly, a shimmer of excitement running through her as the tip of his tongue slowly licked salt and butter from his lower lip.

He chewed appreciatively, seemingly unaware of her touch. "Yum. Stale, oily and oversalted. Perfect movie popcorn."

"Of course. I wanted only the best." She wiped butter and salt from her fingers and offered him a drink of diluted cola, careful to avoid touching him.

"Almost tasteless. Just as I like it," he teased. "Please tell me the mints are old and hard."

"I'm a discriminating gourmet. The mints aren't just old and hard, they're stuck to the side of the box."

"Don't torture me, woman. Feed me bad mints!"

She pried loose several misshapen candies and brought them to his lips. As he took the mints into his mouth, his tongue flicked over her fingertips. Katharine couldn't stop the little "Oh!" she emitted in surprise. Mitch's teasing grin told her the intimate contact was no accident.

She cleared her throat and stepped back. "Since you like action movies, and I like romantic comedies, I compromised and got two romantic comedies."

Mitch rolled his eyes and groaned with exaggeration. "The sacrifices I'll make for bad popcorn."

She inserted *It Happened One Night* into the VCR and settled into the chair. At intervals she rose to give Mitch more popcorn, mints or cola. Each time, she felt a little thrill that came from even the briefest contact with him.

Her attention wandered from the movie on the screen. Mitch was leaving in a week. She was pleased he'd progressed so far in the past two weeks. Naturally, Mitch was elated to escape, as he'd put it. Now he no longer needed her. Perhaps she was one of the things he wanted to escape. She rubbed her icy hands together and shivered.

When *His Girl Friday* ended, Katharine rewound the tapes and discarded the remnants of their theater food. Her face felt stiff as she pushed out a few effusive words.

"Congratulations again, Mitch. This has been a big day in your recovery." Her voice faltered, and she cleared her throat. "I'm glad I got to share in the celebration."

Mitch smiled, but there was no light in his eyes. "You made it a celebration. Thank you," he added softly.

AFTER KATHARINE LEFT, Mitch was surprised that his elation at leaving the hospital was tinged with sadness. After he returned to Houston, he'd see little of Katharine. Since she refused to borrow money from him, nothing would compel her to contact him. Maybe he'd never see or hear from her. Despite the transformation in their relationship, perhaps it was better to end it now. It was time to take up their separate lives again. He wished he could feel content about it, but the prospect of never seeing Katharine again bothered the hell out of him.

Mitch called Francine to inform her of his approaching release from the hospital. "I need a big favor."

"Of course, Mitch, dear. You know I'll help."

"Will you check out rehabilitation facilities for me? I'll send you a list and you can choose one."

Francine paused. "That's a big responsibility, Mitch."

"I know. And I'll need your help during my treatment, too."

"How?"

"I don't know. I'll just need someone who can help me adjust. Who'll encourage me to keep working to get stronger." He loathed the quaver in his voice. "Hell, Francine. I need a friend."

"Well, *of course,* I'm your friend, dear. But you know I'm not very good with sick people."

"Of course."

"I'll inquire about a place for you to stay." Her tone brightened. "I know! I'll hire people to take care of you. I'll call you when the arrangements are made, dear. And I'll come to see you again soon."

"Sure. Goodbye, Francine."

Disappointed but not surprised at his sister's inability to understand his needs, Mitch contemplated his immediate future. His struggle for recovery had just begun. He couldn't begin to envision all that lay ahead. And Katharine wouldn't be with him. There'd be only Francine and the staff she hired.

Feeling chilled, he rang for the nurse, knowing the blanket she placed over him would bring no relief from his icy fear.

5

KATHARINE ENTERED Mitch's room, almost colliding with Francine.

"Nice to see you, Kathie...umm...Katharine." Francine's smile bordered on sincerity.

Startled by her greeting, Katharine managed a weak smile. "You, too, Francine."

Francine patted her hair, then she chattered for a few minutes about her activities.

Katharine's Francine Warning System went on alert. It announced: Francine wants something.

Francine fixed Katharine with a wide-eyed stare. "I'd like to stay in Dallas for a few days and visit with my brother. But with that big convention in town, I can't find a suitable hotel room."

Katharine swallowed her "So what?" and waited, puzzled.

Francine shifted from foot to foot. "Could I ask just the tiniest favor, Katharine? Could I stay at your house? Just for a day or so? You know I won't be any trouble."

Katharine stifled a groan and managed a stiff smile. "My house isn't suitable, either, I'm afraid. I haven't gotten very far with the renovations. The extra bedrooms are furnished with castoffs. I'm the cleaning lady, and I ought to be fired for poor performance."

"I wouldn't have asked you, Katharine, if I'd had a choice. But there simply is not suitable accommodation for me in this town."

It's only for a few days, Katharine told herself. *And Mitch is leaving for Houston soon, so I'll probably never see her again after that.* Her resigned sigh was louder than she intended. "Sure, Francine. Get your things and we'll go."

KATHARINE OPENED HER front door and lugged both of Francine's large suitcases into the foyer. Francine's critical eye took in the cracked tile floor, peeling walls and flaking plaster.

"It needs work," Katharine admitted. "But I love these old prairie-style houses. They're so big and airy."

"And in need of considerable renovation," Francine sniffed.

"Yes, but I enjoy renovating, and a run-down house can be a remarkable bargain," Katharine said, irritated that Francine always made her feel defensive.

Francine responded with an "Umm" and strolled into the dining room that was furnished with a card table, two folding chairs, and an ancient green rug the former owners had left. Her eyes widened at the sight of the large crystal chandelier illuminating the shabby room.

"It's a large enough room," she concluded, then preceded Katharine across the foyer to the living room. "Yes, this is most promising."

Gratified by her sister-in-law's near compliment, Katharine showed her the rest of the house. She couldn't resist assigning Francine to the bedroom furnished with a battered wagon-wheel bed and matching dresser abandoned by the former owners.

While Francine freshened up, Katharine made a simple meal of sandwiches and milk from her poorly stocked refrigerator. Francine joined her in the kitchen. Seating herself carefully on a wobbly chair, Francine thanked Katharine for the food, nibbled daintily for a few moments, then said, "Mitch asked me to find a suitable facility for his recuperation, you know. I went to several of those places in Houston, and I don't mind telling you they're dreadfully depressing."

"Depressing?"

"Oh, yes, dear. They're full of *crippled* people. I don't think it will be good for Mitch to live with people like that."

Katharine quelled her annoyance because Francine was right about Mitch's environment. He hated his existence in the hospital. Living in a rehabilitation center would be much the same. If he lived at home, he'd feel more like he'd rejoined the world. He'd have more opportunity to work. He could easily afford the cost of a staff and transportation to a center for his treatments.

She refilled their milk glasses. "I agree with you. Why don't you arrange for him to live at his house...or yours...?"

"He can't stay at his house. He'd be too lonely."

"Then how about your house?" Katharine persisted.

"I have so much to do, so many obligations, I really can't undertake caring for a sick person." Francine's tone sounded tentative. "It might be best, Katharine, if he stayed in Dallas. He'd be close to his doctor."

"There are good doctors in Houston."

"But Mitch's is the best one. I checked."

Katharine couldn't argue. She'd inquired about Bryson the day after Mitch entered the hospital.

"He really needs a homey atmosphere right here in Dallas so he won't have to make that long trip by ambulance to Houston."

Suddenly Katharine realized where the conversation was headed. She shook her head. "It's impossible, Francine."

"What, dear?"

"Mitch can't stay here."

"But your house is perfect. The dining room could be converted to a bedroom, and the living room would hold all the machines he'll need. The kitchen's just down the hall."

"I'm sure you remember that Mitch and I didn't live well together in the past. I don't think we'd do any better now."

"It won't be the same. He'll just be in your dining room for a while. You'll hardly know he's here. From the looks of things, you don't use those rooms anyway."

"Have you discussed this with Mitch?" Surely he'd veto the idea, she thought.

"Certainly. He thinks it's the best solution."

Mitch *wanted* to stay with her? Katharine's heart pounded. She'd see him every day for months. She felt her resolve fading. "Francine, I have a company to run, a life to lead," she said with less firmness than she'd intended. "I can't take care of Mitch."

"He's your husband. You owe him."

"I don't *owe* him!" she snapped. "I can't take care of him."

"You won't have to. I'll hire a housekeeper for you." She pushed aside her paper plate, wrinkling her nose at the remains of her sandwich. "One who cooks, too. Besides, I was so sure you'd want to help your husband that I leased the equipment and hired the therapists so he won't even have to go out for treatment. Everyone will come here. I'm working on their schedules. All you have to do is see that they do their jobs. That's not much to ask."

"*You what?*" Katharine jumped up and stalked around the kitchen.

"I was so sure you'd want to help poor Mitch, it didn't occur to me that you'd disagree. Everything will be delivered tomorrow."

Francine's lips quivered. "He has no place to go. You're the only one. . . ."

Even in her flustered state, Katharine had to admit that her sister-in-law had a point. Dilapidated though it was, her house would be a convenient place for Mitch, near his doctor.

Katharine threw up her arms in surrender. "Oh, hell! I guess it's okay." She eyed Francine with grudging respect. What a negotiator she was! No wonder the woman had grown much wealthier by successfully divorcing three men.

Francine's woeful expression vanished. "Very well, dear. I'll select a housekeeper tomorrow. Now, it's late, and emotional discussions are so draining. I'll say good-night." She paused in the doorway. "I'm sure you're pleased now that you've agreed to do the right thing for Mitch."

"I'm ecstatic that I've done 'the right thing for Mitch.'"

But have I done the right thing for me? As she cleaned up the kitchen, she realized that, thanks to Francine's meddling, and her own soft heart, Mitch Woods would continue to be a dominant factor in her life for a while longer. Dr. Bryson had been as noncommittal as ever when discussing Mitch's recovery. It could take months—or years. He might regain full strength . . . or not.

During that very trying time for Mitch, he'd be under her roof. Why on earth had he agreed to this arrangement? He'd seemed so intent on returning to Houston. She shrugged at the obvious answer. Once again, she was convenient, and he needed her—for now.

But what would happen to their relationship? They were in limbo now. Where would they end up? They couldn't go back to the old ways. She wouldn't live like that again. But they had no future together because the past was ever present for them. She sighed. She knew what would happen: Eventually Mitch would finish his therapy and return to his life in Houston, and she'd get on with hers.

But how would she control her feelings for him, the desire that coiled through her every time he smiled in a certain way, every time she touched him? She'd just have to avoid being alone with him as much as possible. She'd managed to stay away from the hospital every other day for the past month, but that had required restraint. While he was in her house, she'd be drawn to him. Inevitably.

The absurdity of the situation finally made her smile. She sounded like a Victorian maiden struggling to protect her virtue against an immoral villain who pursued her without mercy. After all, Mitch could hardly overpower her, haul her to bed and ravish her.

He'd never had to physically overpower her, of course. He used simply a look, a touch, a seductive word, and she'd been captivated.

She had to give him credit, though. After the kiss and her explanation of her feelings, he'd treated her as she asked—like a friend. But keeping her distance and fighting the sexual urges that pulsed through her every time they were together were proving to be a formidable challenge.

What had she let herself in for?

BY NOON THE NEXT DAY, several tons of newly assembled equipment occupied Katharine's living room. A hospital bed, a TV and secretarial equipment were set up in her dining room. The old green rug and the card table had disappeared.

When she entered Mitch's room at the hospital, she half expected him to make a "roommate" joke, but he only asked, "How's it going with Francine? You haven't killed her yet, have you?"

"She's her usual overbearing self."

"Did you two manage to talk to each other?"

"Oh, yes. We talked." When Mitch made no comment about her house cum rehab center, Katharine brought up the subject. "Why didn't you tell me about the scheme you and she cooked up?"

Mitch appeared honestly baffled. "Scheme?"

"To turn my house into your therapy center."

"What are you talking about?"

Katharine buried her head in her hands and groaned. "We've been had! Your sister conned me into letting you stay at my house and take your therapy there. She told me you thought it was a good idea!"

"She never said a word! I thought she was finding a place in Houston. Your house? Good Lord!"

"What's wrong with my house? You haven't even seen it! It's perfect!" Katharine stopped abruptly. "Why am I trying to convince you when I thought the idea was crazy?"

"I don't know. Why did you agree?"

Because I want another chance with you! The thought took center stage in her brain. She sought to deny it. She and Mitch were through, and had been for a long time. But he was different now. He treated her with respect, as an equal. He confided in her, relied on her. In the past month they'd begun to know each other, to really like each other—for the first time.

If he stayed at her house, their new rapport might become a deeper relationship—or it might founder. Maybe repairing their battered relationship was a pipe dream. But she'd risk it, even if Mitch ended up disappointing her—hell, hurting her—again.

What if he never gets well? Would he stay with her forever? If he needed her—really depended on her—he'd be unlikely to revert to his old ways. After all, he couldn't run her life from a sickbed. She'd avoid the role of wife—at which she'd failed miserably—and be his friend, his confidante. If Mitch remained disabled, they could have a future together.

Dear God! She'd thought of Mitch's full recovery not as a goal, but as a threat to her future happiness with him. Had she really hoped to tie him to her, make him dependent on her, physically and emotionally, in the name of caring for him?

"Katharine? Are you in there?" Mitch teased.

"I'm sorry. I was thinking."

"I said, 'Thank you for agreeing to put up with me for a while longer.' But I know Francine is as subtle as a steamroller. You can back out, with no hard feelings on my part."

"No. I don't want to back out. Francine was right about my house. There's plenty of room for you and the staff she's hired. It's just a little strange to go from rattling around alone in my house to sharing it with you and a group of strangers." She shrugged. "But I'll adjust. It might be fun."

"At this point guests are supposed to say, 'Don't go to any trouble for me,' but I'll be a hell of a lot of trouble, Katharine."

She saw that Mitch realized staying at her house was as close as he could come to living a normal life for a while.

THE MOVE WENT MORE smoothly than Katharine had expected. Francine bustled about, snapping orders with an efficiency that amazed Katharine. Once Mitch was settled in the dining room, Francine surveyed its tatty interior, her expression a mixture of satisfaction and distaste.

"Mitch, dear, I'm going to call in my designer and have him do this room for you."

"No, you won't!" Katharine interjected.

"These surroundings are depressing," Francine insisted. As she spoke, a low-flying jet rattled the windows and sent a small piece of plaster crashing to the floor.

Katharine rolled her eyes ceilingward and cursed her house for its treason. "I'm the first to admit the place is a mess, Francine. That's why I bought it. *I* want to renovate it. I'm looking forward to climbing up on a ladder and repairing the plaster. *I* want to paint this room, paper it, select the carpet and make the drapes. It's called sweat equity—buying a run-down house and renovating it yourself."

"Mitch," Francine persisted, "you can't live like this."

"Watch me, Francine. I think I'll be very comfortable here." He winked at Katharine like a co-conspirator. "Wondering if the ceiling is going to collapse will take my mind off my problems."

"In the spirit of compromise, Francine," Katharine offered, "I'll stop working on my bathroom and do this room. In my spare time. I'll work around Mitch's schedule, of course." *And*, she added silently, *I can spend as much time in here with Mitch as I want to, but with something harmless to occupy my hands—and mind.*

SATISFIED WITH HER strategy, Francine left for Houston. As Katharine shut the front door behind Francine, she felt uneasy. The nurses, therapists and housekeeper started tomorrow. She and Mitch were alone today—and tonight.

"I have a surprise for you," she said softly. "I'll be right back."

In a few minutes she returned and unfolded a hinged wooden rectangle into a large square painted with small, alternating black-and-white squares. She adjusted wooden legs at each corner until the board stood level a few inches above Mitch's legs.

"A giant chessboard?" he asked incredulously. "Where did you get it?"

"Making stuff out of wood is what I do, Mitch." She opened a box and placed the large chess pieces on the board.

"You made this?"

The awe in his voice was a tonic for her spirits. It pleased her more than any thank-you could have. "To celebrate your escape from the hospital. Want to play?"

"Against myself?"

"I know how," she said quietly. "I've learned to do lots of things in the last three years, Mitch."

"I keep having to learn that, don't I?"

She sat on the bed beside him. "Your move."

"I don't know—my hands are awkward and slow, even with these slings supporting my arms."

She laughed. "Chess isn't a game of speed."

She held her breath as he concentrated on making his arm move and his uncooperative fingers grasp a pawn for his opening gambit.

Pride in his accomplishment glowed in his eyes. "I warn you, I play for blood."

"I don't take prisoners, either. Do your worst."

At dusk, Katharine closed the faded drapes and turned on the chandelier, its soft light painting the room in shades of gold. Still concentrating on their game, they sat together in the warm circle of light, leaving the world outside dark and forgotten.

Katharine reveled in the pleasure of Mitch's company, in the thrill she felt each time they touched, each time their eyes met. *If only this could last. If only we could capture the magic of this moment and make it the rule rather than the exception. If only. . .*

Mitch made a move and quietly announced, "Checkmate."

"Damn."

"You play very well. But I shouldn't be surprised. You do everything well."

Touched by his compliment, she ducked her head. "Thank you, kind sir." She packed the chessmen in their box and folded the board, but stayed seated beside him.

Mitch grinned. "I expect to be properly congratulated, lady. A victory kiss, please."

Katharine hesitated, the memory of their last kiss warming her skin. "A friendly one," she reminded them both. She brushed her lips against his, their gentle warmth tantalizing her for a moment, until he withdrew.

"This one's for my present." He nibbled at her lower lip, his teeth gently teasing, his breath warm across her sensitized skin.

"Mitch."

"And this one's for—" he began, with a raspy hesitance in his voice. "I don't know...." His lips found hers again.

She lifted her head. "Dinner," she whispered and kissed the corner of his mouth.

"Dinner?"

She turned her head and he planted soft damp kisses on her cheek. "I cooked dinner for you."

He nuzzled her earlobe. "Thank you." His breath caressed her ear.

"You're welcome," she murmured. Her vow to avoid touching Mitch passed fleetingly through her mind. But the intimacy of the evening, the pleasure of his kisses, overrode her will.

She turned her mouth to his. "Very welcome." She closed her eyes, concentrating on the tantalizing feel of Mitch's mouth against hers. His tongue probed between her lips and she opened her mouth, inviting him to explore.

They shared a slow, searching kiss that left Katharine shivery.

Too soon, he drew away. "That was more than friendly, Kat."

"Umm." She nuzzled his stubbled cheek against hers, then sought his lips.

Mitch groaned softly. "God, how I hate to say this."

"What?"

"Not tonight, dear. I'm too tired. You'd better go to bed."

Katharine caught her lower lip between her teeth, both disappointed and relieved that Mitch had called a halt. "You're right." She sighed. "Let me help turn you first." She removed his arms from the slings, then rotated his back and legs so that he lay on his side. "I'll come back every two hours."

Katharine adjusted the sheet and plumped his pillow. "Good night, Mitch."

"Kiss me like that again sometime, friend." A devilish glint showed in his eyes. "Soon."

TRUE TO HER WORD, Katharine returned to shift him to his back. After another two hours she turned him to his side. She moved quickly, efficiently—longing all the while to caress him. Acknowledging the risk, she lay down beside him, on top of the blanket so their bodies wouldn't touch, yet close enough that she felt the heat of him. She savored the sweet torture until it was time to return him to his back. Then she went alone to her big, cold bed.

6

A LOUD, JANGLING DOORBELL jolted Mitch awake. He heard Katharine stumble through the foyer and fling open the door. In a moment she parted the sliding doors of the dining room and a matronly woman carrying a small suitcase walked in.

"Mr. Woods, I'm Gloria from the agency. I'll be bathing and grooming you every morning until you can do it yourself."

He had grown accustomed to the necessity of being bathed like an infant. Now, if Kat were bathing him, he might grow to enjoy it.

A few minutes later, the doorbell shrilled again. The housekeeper-cook arrived with three suitcases, so he assumed she would live in. She immediately took charge in the kitchen and prepared the first tasty breakfast he'd had in months. Then the day nurse came on duty, asked him a series of questions, checked his vital signs, and pronounced him none the worse for the stress of the move.

At nine, Katharine ushered in Steve, the physical therapist. Mitch scrutinized the slightly built man who appeared to be in his mid-thirties, close to his own age.

Mitch realized he'd spend innumerable hours working with this man, following his instructions. Mitch's chance to rebuild his body depended upon this therapist's skill. A knot tightened in his belly. He hoped to hell Steve knew what he was doing. Wanting to hide his apprehension, he boomed an effusive, "Hello."

Steve returned the greeting, briefed Mitch and Katharine on his background, then asked Mitch a few questions. Next, he produced a transfer board.

Mitch gritted his teeth as Steve manipulated him via the transfer board onto a gurney. Another way to be stripped of his dignity, he thought. One of thousands. But his irritation was short-lived as Steve pushed him across the room and through the foyer; the gurney provided a kind of freedom! He grimaced. His definition of freedom certainly had shrunk since GBS began dominating his life.

When they reached the living room/rehab center, Steve explained each exercise and its purpose. Then he grasped Mitch's hand. "I want to feel your grip. Squeeze as hard as you can for as long as you can."

Mitch stared at his hand, commanding the muscles to move. He held his breath while his fingers bent only slightly, so he redoubled his effort until he felt sweat beading on his upper lip. Exhausted, he muttered, "Damn!" and let his hand go slack.

"Take it easy, Mitch," Katharine teased. "This isn't the Olympic trials. It's rehab."

"I've got no strength."

Steve shook his head vigorously. "You're stronger than you think. You can grip, and that's a good sign. You also have some movement in your arms. Another good sign. I can help you."

"How long will it take?"

"As long as it takes. We have to retrain your muscles. It won't be easy. And I'll work your butt off. I can't exercise for you, but I'll make you do it. You'll want to give up, but I won't let you." His voice was low and calm, yet determined.

"So you believe in challenging your patients?" Katharine asked.

"Not all of them, Ms. Drake. But him—definitely." He smiled confidently at Mitch. "And it'll work because I figure you can't resist a challenge."

Mitch knew he'd been tagged. "You're right. And I won't give up until you do. I'm going to show you."

His gaze met Katharine's, and he added in a softer tone, "And you, too." Without waiting for her response, he barked at Steve, "Let's get started."

"I'll leave you gentlemen to your work, and I'll go attend to mine," Katharine told them.

Steve watched her leave, and when she was out of earshot he commented, "First-class lady. Is she a relative?"

"She's my wife," Mitch said briskly, wanting to prevent further discussion.

"You're kidding."

"No." Mitch frowned.

Steve paused, then winked. "Why didn't you say so? I can order a wider bed for you."

"No, thanks."

"Look, man, if you've experienced impotence, well... It's not usually a long-term problem with GBS. The chances are good that you can perform again after a while."

For a moment, Mitch itched to discuss his sexual fears—his terrible anxiety over whether he could sustain an erection and reach climax—and more important, to express his feelings about Katharine, his regrets. But Steve was a stranger.

"No. We're separated. I'm really here by circumstance."

Steve shrugged. "Whatever you say."

PLEASED BY STEVE'S professionalism and the spontaneous rapport developing between him and Mitch, Katharine went upstairs to her office. She ate lunch between phone calls to Gus and Art Harris, while sifting through invoices.

Although she'd hoped to escape the pandemonium caused by the new people in her house, the housekeeper interrupted Katharine several times, needing her assistance in finding things. She'd get used to the new people soon enough. After all, the woman was already reintroducing the concepts of regular meals, cleanliness and order to the domestic confusion Katharine normally lived in.

Since tomorrow was the end of the month, she wrote paychecks for her employees, paid bills, and then reviewed her finances. The bank balance kept shrinking. She shivered and rubbed her upper arms to warm them.

She had to find an investor, but Art Harris kept reporting dead ends in his search for prospects. Knowing it was fruitless to analyze the depressing numbers any further, she made phone calls to order lumber, trim, and varnish. More bills to pay.

Restless, she bounded downstairs. As she approached the dining room, her antique doorbell rang, announcing the arrival of the occupational therapist.

A couple of hours later she checked to see if Mitch was free, but discovered his part-time secretary taking notes while he conducted a conference-call meeting on his speaker phone.

At five, the night nurse arrived. Katharine sighed at the relative quiet and approached Mitch's room. The nurse met her at the door, her finger to her lips. "He's very tired, Ms. Drake," she whispered. "He's had an unsettling day. I'd rather you didn't wake him."

"It's okay. He needs to rest." As she trudged upstairs to her bedroom, Katharine smiled wryly. She remembered how she'd been worried about being alone with Mitch, about the increased risk of igniting the sexual desire that sparked between them. With six other people coming and going every day, she'd have to make an appointment to see him.

Pausing only for a good stretch to ease her tense muscles, Katharine sank onto her bed. In too few hours Gloria would ring the doorbell and start another day.

ON THE THIRD MORNING Gloria's arrival was announced by a lilting chime. More like a carillon, Katharine thought groggily as she rushed downstairs. Someone had replaced her old doorbell! She glared at the door of Mitch's room.

After Mitch had had his bath, Katharine confronted him, asking testily, "Did you have my doorbell changed?"

"I replaced it with a twentieth-century version," he said, looking as if he expected applause. "You certainly needed one, so I called in the order."

He'd been in her house for two days and already was taking charge. Same old Mitch. She clamped her lips together to control her anger, barely managing to speak calmly. "I'm sure you meant well, but please don't buy gifts for me, or for my house."

"Don't you like the sound? I thought it was an improvement."

"The sound is fine, but that's not the point. As I managed to impress on Francine, *I* want to redo my house when I have time and money."

"Then don't think of it as a gift to you. I bought it to save my hearing—and sanity," he quipped.

He failed to understand her message, she realized. Short of ripping the chimes off the wall and stomping on them, which would hardly solve the real problem between them, there was little she could do to further emphasize that she wanted to make her own decisions—even small ones.

ON SATURDAY MORNING, almost a week after Mitch's arrival, Katharine came up with a safe way to spend time with him. She donned an old pair of sweats and tied a bandanna over her hair. Then she hauled her stepladder and supplies into Mitch's room, covered the office equipment with a drop cloth, climbed the ladder, and began pulling pieces of cracked plaster from the twelve-foot ceiling.

Even from her distant perch she could see the definition of Mitch's arm muscles, already growing stronger under Steve's supervision. She concentrated her attention on the ceiling to keep her eyes off Mitch, who lay bare chested and sweaty after his daily therapy session. A sheet and light blanket draped him from the waist down. She wondered if he was naked beneath the covers. She sneaked a speculative peek at his midsection, then blushed when she found him watching her.

He appeared unaware of her discomfort. "I need your help, Katharine."

Since Mitch was rarely so forthright about asking for assistance, she was especially curious. "What can I do?"

"I need to pay for some stuff. Sam is authorized to sign checks for the company, but not for my personal account. My secretary prepared them, and you can sign them."

"And face a forgery rap?"

"Your name is still on the signature card."

Startled that she could use their old joint-checking account, given all their quarrels about money, she asked sharply, "Why?"

"I never changed the arrangement."

"Surely you didn't intend to continue supporting me," she said dryly.

Mitch shifted his gaze and seemed embarrassed. "I planned to keep tabs on you by what you spent and where."

Of course, he wouldn't be motivated by generosity. Irritated by his intent to monitor her activities, she snapped, "It never occurred to me to use your account!" She pried off a loose piece of plaster with unnecessary force, sending it crashing to the floor near Mitch's bed.

"I know that now! Don't stone me, I'm a changed man!"

And I'm the queen of Transylvania, she thought. "Sure, I'll sign your checks after I'm finished here."

"You ought to have my credit cards, too."

"I might lose control and spend a bundle," she retorted waspishly.

"No, you won't," he replied with quiet confidence.

With the loose plaster cleared from a two-foot area, Katharine mixed water into the dry plaster powder, stirred it into a thick cream, then remounted the ladder. Working slowly, she pressed the plaster against the wood laths. The sharp metal studs in the laths, intended to hold the plaster in place, bit into her fingers and palms.

Mitch watched her work for a while, then asked, "How do you find the time and energy to work on this huge old place?"

"It's cheap entertainment. I can have lots of fun with ten dollars' worth of plaster or paint. Besides, I'm an 'urban pioneer,' rebuilding an old house in the inner city. At first I planned to fix it up, sell it and reap a huge profit as others have done. But I fell in love with this old place, and now I want to keep it." She pressed more plaster into place, smoothed it, then examined her work critically.

"How big is your house? I've only seen this room, the foyer and the living room."

"Downstairs there's also a kitchen, breakfast room, and two other rooms. I haven't decided what to do with them yet. Upstairs there's a master suite with a bathroom and sitting room, four other bedrooms, and two bathrooms."

"That's a lot of space for one person."

"I admit it looks as if I'm getting ready for Ward Cleaver to show up so we can live happily ever after with a swarm of cheerful kids."

"I thought you didn't want kids. Not mine, anyway."

Remembering the uncertainties and inadequacies she'd experienced during the years with Mitch broke her good mood. She'd always wanted children, but her relationship with Mitch had been so unstable, she'd feared bringing a child into a marriage that was heading nowhere. "It wouldn't have been a good idea for us to have children," she said stiffly.

"It might have helped."

Mitch sounded a bit wistful, she thought. But she refused to sentimentalize their past. She remembered *exactly* the way things had been between them. "It would have been a real mess if we'd had children—considering what's happened to us."

Apparently Mitch thought it wise not to pursue that topic any further. "So, are you expecting Ward Cleaver?" he asked, changing the subject.

"I've given up waiting for him. It's foolish to put my life on hold until he shows up. As soon as I can afford it, I'm going to adopt."

"You mean be a single parent? Will agencies accept you?"

"Not if I want a perfect, white infant. There's a long line of Ward-and-Junes who get preference for those babies."

She continued speaking as she applied more plaster. "But there are many other children who need loving parents, or even a single parent. There are agencies that specialize in adoptions of orphaned children from South America, Africa, Southeast Asia. An unmarried friend of mine adopted two babies from Peru."

Unsure why she needed Mitch's approval, Katharine continued to justify herself, feeling more and more defensive. "I think I'll be a good mother. I'll have to work extra hard at it, since there'll be only me."

"You've really thought this through, haven't you?"

"As soon as I can afford it, I'll sign up." She stopped working for a minute, but kept her gaze on the ceiling.

"I know I'll miss out on giving birth, but most of my friends claim pregnancy is overrated. It's the bonding—the love, the nurturing of a child—that makes you a parent." Her voice cracked and Katharine felt embarrassed for getting so emotional in front of Mitch. "I hope they're right." She pretended to study her handiwork while she calmed herself.

Katharine had never confided her dreams to anyone. Why had she chosen to bare her soul to Mitch after all these years? Probably she still harbored some foolish hope that he would suddenly transform himself into Ward and promise her respect, undying devotion and all the babies she wanted. Fat chance!

She turned to a more neutral topic. "How do you feel about your therapy?"

"It's slow. I can hardly tell any difference."

From her perch, Katharine checked out his body again. She could see a definite improvement as her gaze caressed his shoulders and chest. "Steve's pleased with your progress."

"He's not living in my body. From in here, it feels like nothing's happening." He shut his eyes and drew a rasping breath. "And there's the damnable not knowing."

He looked so frustrated that she climbed down the ladder and went over to soothe him.

"Dr. Bryson says all the signs are good, Mitch."

"I know. But it's the uncertainty—not knowing how much I can recover or how long it will take."

He cursed emphatically. "You don't have to put up with me, you know. I must be driving you crazy."

"You always did. But this time you brought a retinue to help send me over the brink. I might as well be of some use in the meantime. Where are those checks for me to sign?"

Feeling like an imposter, Katharine wrote "Mrs. Mitchell J. Woods" on the signature line of a dozen checks.

KATHARINE PULLED the secretary's chair beside the bed and sat next to Mitch. He was pleased when she took his hand and rubbed her fingers over the back of it. "Don't let this get you down, Mitch. If you weren't frustrated by your situation, you'd have to be crazy. But remember, you vowed to show Steve . . . and me."

Mitch relaxed as Katharine gently massaged his hand, but after a few moments he realized something was wrong. Katharine's hands, usually firm and smooth, felt rough against his skin. "What's wrong with your hands?" he demanded, concerned that she'd hurt herself.

She raised her hands—her palms and fingers were covered with scratches, punctures and bruises. "Plastering is nasty work," she said lightly.

"Why didn't you wear gloves?"

"They get in my way."

"But you hurt yourself!"

"I like the feeling of soft, smooth plaster against rough wood. I think it's called tactile satisfaction, or some such thing. I like working with my hands."

"Surely you can get your tactile satisfaction doing something less painful?"

"A dab of first-aid cream will take care of the scratches. It requires some blood, sweat and tears to be an urban pioneer."

He didn't know this new Katharine—this woman who confronted life head-on, who found joy and pride in doing work most people spurned or avoided. A woman who set her own course, who could survive without him or any man in her life. Not even to father her children, he thought grimly.

"I hope you're rebuilding the house as well as you've rebuilt your life, Kat." His wistful tone annoyed him. "You're sure working on it."

"And paying a price," she added softly, splaying her hands as evidence.

Mitch thought of the price she'd paid to rebuild her life: himself. She'd had to leave him to have the life she wanted.

He tried lifting her hands to his lips and was gratified that she helped him. He brought her palms against his cheeks, then kissed each one.

He drew a deep breath. There were things he needed to talk about, things they'd buried years ago. "I'm sorry I made you so unhappy when we were married—umm—together. I never meant to hurt you. I didn't know I had until you told me that night at the hospital."

"I never thought you wanted to hurt me. But you did."

Her eyes darkened for a moment, and he wondered if she was remembering those painful times, and if she was still hurting.

"But that's all over now." She slowly withdrew her hands from his face.

He wanted to ask her to stay close, to touch him, but he couldn't. He'd agreed to be only her friend, and he'd keep his promise. Yet, she'd seemed about to open up, to talk for the first time about their failure.

"What did I do?"

She hesitated for a moment. "It's what you didn't do," she said. "You never respected me as an individual. You treated me like an ornament, something beautiful attached to you at the elbow. My role was to be at your beck and call, to be your hostess. I was supposed to look pretty, dress well, be charming to your guests, and keep my opinions to myself."

He saw resentment flare in her eyes. But he nonetheless felt compelled to bring up his own frustrations. "It wasn't all my fault, you know. You weren't perfect, either. You never gave me the support I needed."

Katharine rose and began pacing. He didn't want to hurt her, but he had to continue his explanation. "I wanted you to understand why I came home late or shut myself in the study. I was in the process of expanding the company— I was taking a big risk when I added the first three new distribution centers."

And, after she'd left him, he'd driven himself even harder, unwilling to slow down because working kept his mind off her.

Katharine faced him from across the room. "You're right," she admitted huskily. "I never considered my own failings. It was easier to blame you, I guess."

"I wanted you to be happy as my wife. I couldn't understand why all I gave you wasn't enough. You were actively involved with several charities. Those activities took up a lot of time, and I hoped you'd be satisfied."

"I did those things because you wanted me to. Because it was expected of Mrs. Mitchell Woods. Because your mother had been one of Houston's best-known socialites, everyone expected me to be like her and Francine. You grew up in that world and were used to it, but it was all so new, so foreign to me. The people were *your* friends. I tried to fit in, but I never felt comfortable."

"I thought you'd like working for charities. You're a pretty soft touch, you know."

"I'm not criticizing your mother's or Francine's charity work. But I like a more hands-on approach to helping people. One reason I'm pushing so hard to produce the playground equipment is that once I recoup expenses, I can form a nonprofit corporation and donate equipment to schools and public parks."

"Like you gave away art supplies to impoverished students?"

"I was pretty naive, wasn't I? I really believed my store would succeed. All I had to do was open the doors in the morning and money would pour in." A rueful smile tilted the corners of her mouth. "I could have used some guidance from, oh, say, a successful businessman, perhaps."

He knew she was right. He could have helped her. He drew a deep breath. "I thought you were just a little immature, that you'd give up on business when you found out that you'd have to work hard." Acknowledging the flimsiness of his excuses, he suddenly felt ashamed.

"You thought I'd grow up and accept your version of how I should live my life?"

"It was good enough for Francine and my mother— My God, Kat! I was trying to make you into the kind of wife my mother was."

He saw shock register in her eyes. "Your *mother?*"

"She was a warmer, more caring version of Francine. She loved charity functions, luncheons with her friends, shopping for clothes, and entertaining for Dad."

Silently they stared at each other. He'd tried to make vivacious, witty, competent, complex Katharine into someone like his mother, who had lived her life through her husband, who had no goals of her own. Why had he thought that was a good idea?

Katharine mimicked Francine's hand-wringing posture and drawl. "But, Mitch, dear, it simply didn't work, now did it, dear?"

Mitch laughed, breaking the tension. "It makes sense in a weird sort of way. You and I should have talked about some basic matters, like life-styles, before we married."

"While we talked about careers and commitments, you could have courted me with flowers and perfume," she teased.

"You're right, but I didn't have time." He hated the persistent, defensive tone in his voice. "Our courtship lasted about three hours at Tim and Janet's wedding reception, then we made love for the whole weekend and got engaged. We married within a month. No time for frills."

"I'd have liked being courted," she mused.

"I should have given you those things. I should have done a lot of things differently."

He felt her pulling back emotionally, distancing herself. "There's an old saying," she said crisply: "'We grow too soon old and too late smart.' We're too late smart, aren't we, Mitch?"

Mitch's heart sank. Again she confirmed what he'd *once* wanted to hear—that they couldn't salvage the past. When had that truth started to hurt so much?

Right now, he desperately needed to be alone, to regain his equilibrium. "I'm tired, Katharine. I need to sleep."

"Should I turn you on your back before I go?"

He wanted her to touch him, wanted to feel her hands on him—hands he knew would caress his skin. But her touch would only inflame him.

"No," he said sharply, then forced a lighter tone. "I've learned a new trick. Watch." Concentrating, he slowly tipped his shoulder backward until momentum and gravity combined to pull him onto his back. "Great mobility, huh?"

Katharine applauded. "Great, indeed." She hauled her ladder and equipment into the foyer. "Good night, Mitch." She turned off the light and closed the double doors.

He stared at the darkened ceiling and acknowledged his emotions. He was falling in love with his wife again. But this time it was different. He was attracted to her not simply because she was beautiful and sexy, but because of all the other things she was—bright, witty, independent, self-reliant, warm, caring, generous. The list of adjectives rolled on.

He wanted to tell her how he felt. He wanted to see joy in her eyes, hear her encourage him. But if he told her, and she rebuffed him—and who could blame her?—the pain of her rejection would wound him immeasurably.

But that wasn't the greatest risk. He no longer believed she was after his money. But would she truly grow to love him, or would she just pity him? Out of a sense of duty to her husband, despite all that had gone before?

No, he vowed. He'd never tie her to him and his uncertain future when she was so happy to be free. Free of him.

He'd keep his own counsel and demonstrate his love through his actions instead of words.

Too late smart.

7

KATHARINE SMILED AS Mitch demonstrated his new wheelchair. He'd come a long way in the six weeks since he'd left the hospital, but only because of his extraordinary effort, she knew. Yet, even now, underlying the jubilation in his eyes were traces of frustration that he wasn't recovering faster.

"Before GBS, only a Ferrari sports car could give me the thrill that matches the way I feel about this chair." Haltingly, he lifted his arms and patted the narrow fenders, his movements still slow, unsure.

"Is there some connection with the blue van in the driveway? I almost ran into it."

"I leased it as soon as I found out about the wheelchair. It means I can get out of here! So long as you'll load me in and out of the van...and drive. Steve showed me all the stuff today. He'll come in early tomorrow, before you leave for work, and show you."

I can get out of here, her mind repeated, as a cold chill brought goose bumps to her skin. He wanted his freedom now as badly as she'd wanted hers three and a half years ago. And when he got it, she would be hurt just as badly.

"You look like you're ready to go cruising. I should put the women of Dallas on notice," she said, forcing herself to sound cheerful.

"You can't imagine how caged in I've felt since I've been sick—three long months—because you get to go out every day. Lord knows, I'm ready to go."

Seeing the animation in his face, she shoved aside her gloomy thoughts of the future, and vowed to enjoy the present. From his expression she guessed that he had the same idea as she did. "Do you think we can do it?" she asked tentatively.

"We're reasonably intelligent adults. Sure we can. Steve said he'd give us some advice, but I know we can figure it out."

"Where will we go?"

"A movie and dinner. Ready?"

"Sure. I've still got my coat on." She thought they sounded like kids conspiring to run away from home. "I'll get your sport coat."

Mitch handled the chair's battery-powered controls awkwardly, but kept the chair on course through the foyer and out the door Katharine held open. He rolled onto the porch, then braked suddenly.

Puzzled, Katharine blurted, "What's the matter?" Then she saw the cracked, uneven steps. Four of them.

"*Dammit!* I'm still trapped!"

"I can get you down the stairs, and back up. My college roommate broke her leg skiing and I helped her get around the campus in a wheelchair."

"Are you sure?"

"Of course," she said with more confidence than she felt. "Wipe that dubious look off your face. We can do this."

"Honey, you don't weigh a hundred pounds soaking wet. I don't want you to hurt yourself. I'll just sit out here for a while and enjoy the fresh air and the sunset."

Irked by his paternal attitude and unwilling to admit defeat, she grasped the handles and guided him to the top of the steps before tilting the chair backward so that most of the weight rested on the wheels. Cautiously she lowered the chair down the steps, straining every muscle to control the heavy, unwieldly load.

She heard his apprehensive gasp and realized he must be frightened. If she lost control of the wheelchair, he'd fall down the stairs, unable to protect himself against injury. Each step jarred him and she muttered assurances as her arm muscles burned with the strain.

Mitch chuckled nervously. "I'll bet the thing Steve tells us is, 'Make sure you have a ramp.'"

Finally, with Mitch and the chair safely on the sidewalk, Katharine heaved a great sigh. "I'd better call and make sure of a couple of other details before we leave."

She returned in a few minutes and announced, "I'd forgotten the term 'wheelchair accessible,' but I located a restaurant and a theater that can accommodate us." She walked beside him as he guided the chair to the side of the van.

"What movie?"

"Mel Gibson's latest. Lots of action for you—" she grinned slyly "—and lots of Mel for me."

His hearty laugh at her joke demonstrated his exhilaration at his newfound freedom.

With Mitch giving instructions, she lowered the lift, locked the chair in place, and raised it into the van.

She reversed the procedure successfully at the Lakewood Theatre, but didn't relax until they got inside and Mitch was parked at the end of the last row where an aisle seat had been removed. The overhead lights were still on and people were scurrying up the aisle toward the snack bar.

Katharine watched people stare at the chair, then at Mitch, and finally at her, pity obvious on their faces. Some shook their heads sadly before looking away. But Mitch stared straight ahead, as if the blank screen held endless fascination. She noticed a muscle twitching in his neck.

Steve probably intended to warn us about facing strangers, too, she thought. The stares upset her, but she knew it must be much worse for Mitch—the object of their insensitive pity.

Offering reassurance, she intertwined her fingers with his and was gratified when he slowly curved his fingers and squeezed the back of her hand. The intimate touch and the feeling that the two of them were allied against the world made Katharine feel defiant and proud to be with him.

Mercifully, the lights dimmed and the movie started. Katharine slipped out to the snack bar and bought their favorite treats. She set a box of buttery popcorn on his lap and popped several pieces into his mouth. She grasped the cola cup firmly in her greasy hands, then lifted it toward Mitch. When the cup began sliding, the straw slipped from Mitch's lips and fell into his lap. They giggled and whispered until a patron turned around and hissed, "Shh!"

When the end credits began to roll, Katharine was determined to hold Mitch's attention so that he'd avoid any of the audience's departing appraisals.

"Mitch?" He turned his head to face her, and she launched into a monologue of inane comments about the movie.

He listened attentively, then nodded in agreement with her lame analysis of the redeeming value of the film. "Any movie with Mel Gibson in it can't be all bad," she concluded.

She lowered her lashes and surveyed the aisle. Finally the theater had emptied. "Dinnertime."

A RESTAURANT EMPLOYEE smoothly lowered Mitch's chair down two steps, and the maître d' showed them to their table. Mitch's approving glance around the elegant dining room pleased Katharine.

"This is great," he said. "The Mansion on Turtle Creek is one of Dallas's best restaurants. Tonight I'd have been satisfied with Bubba's Burger Bar."

"I've never been here before," she volunteered. "I've been saving it for a special occasion." She raised her water glass in a toast. "This is a very special occasion."

She sought to quell her doubts. Of course, it was special. Mitch had made a significant step in his recovery, and she was glad for him. He was so happy to have more freedom; so happy to be a little closer to returning to his old life. And she'd return to hers. The prospect of a new separation made her shiver with dread, and she ran her palms up and down her arms.

"Why the bleak look?"

"I should have worn a heavier sweater. I'm a little chilled."

The waiter appeared, handing an opened menu to Katharine, then Mitch. He reached haltingly for it with both hands but couldn't grasp the thin edges. Unobtrusively, the waiter lay the menu on the table before Mitch, announced the evening's specials, then disappeared.

"We forgot something, Katharine." The dismay in his voice was obvious.

"We did?"

"What am I going to eat? The nurses still feed me, except for raw carrots and celery. They're not on the menu. God, how stupid!"

"Your back is to the room, so no one will know if you're a little messy," she assured him. "We'll think of something."

"Forget it. I can't handle anything more complicated than a grilled cheese. Even though my French is lousy, I know sandwich *au fromage grillé* isn't on the menu."

"The chef can handle a special order, and I'll have the same," she insisted as the waiter approached.

"Okay. Here goes," he whispered, then addressed the waiter in his take-charge tone. "The lady will have a grilled-cheese sandwich, and so will I."

The waiter maintained his imperious manner. "Very well, *monsieur,* I'll speak to the chef."

The wine steward approached. Before he presented the wine list, Mitch said, "A Dom Pérignon champagne. The seven-year-old, if you have it." His gaze caught hers and held it with compelling intensity. "This is a special occasion," he said fervently. After a moment, he turned back to the steward and instructed, "Serve mine in a large, bottom-heavy glass with a straw, and the lady's in your finest flute."

The candlelight highlighted the planes of Mitch's cheeks, the firm angle of his jaw, and the warmth of his eyes. She wanted to touch his face, feel the slightly abrasive stubble over smooth, taut skin. Instead, she

covered his hand with hers, seeking to re-create the ca-
maraderie they'd shared in the movie theater.

"Kathie? Kathie?" a female voice interrupted.

Katharine jerked her gaze to the woman who'd
paused at Mitch's elbow. It was one of her college
friends who was now a buyer for a furniture store in af-
fluent North Dallas.

"Ellen. How nice to see you," she lied.

The woman glanced from Katharine to Mitch and
back again. "I thought you two were divorced."

"Separated," Mitch and Katharine said in toneless
unison.

"But now you're back together. How romantic."

"No," each responded firmly.

Standing slightly behind Mitch, Ellen glanced at the
wheelchair. "I'm on the way to the powder room,
Kathie. Come with me. I haven't seen you in ages."

Before Katharine could decline, Mitch suggested
quietly, "Go ahead. I'll be fine."

She rose and followed Ellen. Katharine barely cleared
the door to the ladies' room when Ellen burst out,
"What happened to Mitch?"

Katharine briefly explained GBS.

"But you're not reconciled?"

"No."

Ellen placed a delicate hand to her throat. "No, of
course not. You wouldn't saddle yourself with
a . . . handicapped person."

"His illness wasn't the cause of our separation, Ellen. It won't have any effect on it." She wasn't about to supply details for the heartrending story Ellen seemed to expect. She refused to pander to her appetite for gossip.

"I'd like to see you more often, Kathie," Ellen insisted. "We used to have so much fun. Remember when we were in school and we cut classes for a week to go to Hawaii with those guys we met in the student center? Of course, you got mad because you wound up with the homely one, and he hardly talked at all!"

Recalling the "fun," Katharine shuddered inwardly. She'd made jokes about that earnest, shy young man, mainly to entertain Ellen. Now she felt disgusted with herself over her casual disregard for others' feelings.

Anxious to get away from Ellen, she said, "Let's have lunch soon and talk about furniture." She excused herself and hurried out of the powder room. Weaving her way back to the table, she marveled at Ellen's shallowness. The woman's blithe conclusion that Katharine would reject Mitch because of physical disabilities infuriated her. Yet, Ellen had reminded her how superficial and thoughtless she herself had once been.

Jolted by the realization, she wondered if Mitch's impressions of her had been valid when they married. He'd admitted he had thought she was immature. Had he been right? Had it taken her these last three years to outgrow her immaturity, her self-centeredness?

She'd never tried to understand why work was so important to him. Rather, she'd resented doing her part to support his efforts. She'd regarded entertaining his business acquaintances and friends as a burden rather than a pleasure. She began to realize she'd owed him a greater effort at fitting into his life. When they'd talked about their marriage several weeks ago, she'd recognized the validity of some of his points. But she'd convinced herself that time and rejection had made him exaggerate her faults. Suddenly she saw that he'd been right: She'd contributed as much—or as little—to their unsatisfying marriage as he had.

"I'm sorry," she murmured, as she eased into the chair next to his. He'd think she was referring to her brief absence, but she was apologizing for much more.

"It's okay. I survived without you."

And planned to continue doing so, she thought remorsefully.

The waiter served their grilled-cheese sandwiches with aplomb, but the wine steward paled when he poured expensive champagne into a large glass for Mitch.

Mitch's fingers fumbled as he tried to pick up the sandwich. Katharine placed it in his hands and he nodded gratefully. They ate slowly, as though the sandwiches were gourmet cuisine to be savored, and sipped the champagne with genuine appreciation.

The elegant restaurant, the soft music and the fine wine were a painful reminder of the closeness they'd experienced so long ago. Why hadn't they shared more moments like this? Why hadn't they tried harder?

When the waiter returned to refill the glasses, Katharine declined, "No, thanks. I'm driving."

"*Monsieur?*"

Mitch glanced at the wheelchair. "No, thanks. I'm driving, too. But we'd like to take the bottle with us."

Katharine reached for her purse.

"This one's on me, Kat. Use my credit card."

"No. This dinner is *my* treat," she insisted.

The waiter took the credit card Katharine placed on the table.

"He probably thinks recorking fine champagne is a form of alcohol abuse," Mitch commented.

As Katharine calculated the tip, she noticed the date imprinted on the credit-card slip. November fifteenth.

Today was their seventh wedding anniversary. She glanced at Mitch through lowered lashes, and felt an intense sadness.

WITH THE HELP of the night nurse, Katharine transferred Mitch to his bed. As they helped him slip off his jacket and shirt, he held each arm away from his body while she tugged the sleeves down. His control over the long muscles in his arms had improved noticeably in the last weeks. When he was settled, she adjusted the head of the bed to a comfortable semireclining angle. Then she dismissed the nurse for the evening.

"Let's finish the champagne," he suggested.

She went into the kitchen and returned with two glasses. After pouring the wine, she raised her glass in a toast, then sat beside him on the bed.

He sipped his champagne through a straw. "Thank you for a lovely evening, Ms. Drake."

She chuckled. "As staged by the Three Stooges. It was fun, wasn't it? Like going out on a date."

Mitch's playful expression turned solemn. "I can't tell you what tonight meant to me, Kat. It was a taste of freedom that you gave me. And you did all the work. I meant what I said. Thank you for the lovely evening, Kat."

Remembering the pitying stares, she wanted to talk about Mitch's feelings. "I wasn't prepared for . . . people."

Mitch groaned. "I'd never considered that people would look at me differently if I was in a wheelchair. I hated those looks. The kids were the worst at first, because they were so obvious about it—so blatantly curious. Then I realized they're at least honest. The adults were shocked and would look away for an instant, but they couldn't resist looking again. That's when I'd see their damn pity!"

Katharine slipped her palm across his and noticed that his fingers curved over the back of her hand, ex-

erting a light pressure—more evidence that he was regaining strength.

"I know it's lousy for you," she said firmly, "but you'd
better get used to it—for a while, at least. You loved
getting out, and you'll want to do it again."

"Count on it."

"People aren't going to change. They'll stare at anyone with a physical handicap. Everyone does. I've done
it, Mitch—exactly as you said." She shook her head.
"But I certainly won't do it again."

"God knows, neither will I. And you're right. I have
to get used to it. For a while, though. Just for a while.
But you've treated me like a normal person since the
beginning."

"You *are* normal. Maybe more normal than before,"
she added, grinning. All she could think about was her
urge to touch him, kiss him. She was falling in love with
Mitch all over again. She leaned over him and brushed
his mouth with hers.

His lips were firm and warm, and tasted of champagne. She and Mitch had only the present; but tonight, the present was enough.

Mitch groaned with pleasure. She stretched out beside him and wrapped his arm around her waist. The
heat of his body drew her closer, engulfed her. She
stroked his chest, loving the feel of supple skin and crisp
hair over hard muscle.

Katharine kissed him again and Mitch responded eagerly. She wanted to make love to him, to bring him the release he needed so desperately.

"Oh, Kat, I'm aching to see you, touch you. All of you."

She rose to her knees and unbuttoned her sweater slowly, watching Mitch watch her. The desire flaring in his eyes aroused her. She slipped the garment from her shoulders and down her arms. Then she skimmed the soft wool across Mitch's bare belly, making his flesh quiver.

Her fingers trembling, she lifted the hem of her camisole. The caress of soft silk on her breasts made her nipples tighten. She pulled off the filmy garment with both hands and held it above her head. She closed her eyes, arched her back, and stretched sinuously, fully aware of the seductive impact her pose would have on Mitch.

"Ah, Kat. Hurry. Please."

She shed the rest of her clothing, feeling oddly shy to be naked and vulnerable before him after so long.

His appreciative sigh reassured her.

"So beautiful," he whispered.

She straddled his upper thighs. The head of his bed was elevated so that mere inches separated their faces and torsos. Cupping his hands in hers, she guided them to her breasts and watched as he took their weight in his palms. His thumbs stroked her nipples, and the slight abrasive pressure brought the sensitized tips to hard peaks. She gasped at the exquisite pleasure that raced like electricity through her.

She let her fingers tease down his chest and belly. Her lips followed, pausing as she flicked her tongue into his navel, then sucked at it. He gasped.

"Stop, Kat. Now." His words were little more than an erotic moan.

"I want us to do this," she insisted.

"Oh, sweetheart, so do I. But if you keep that up, I'll explode."

"That was my plan."

"I want to please you. I have to know if I still can. Help me."

Trembling with need, pent-up emotion restricting her breath, Katharine took his hands and placed them at her waist. Her skin warmed from his touch.

Mitch moved his hand down her belly. His fingers smoothed her coppery curls, then gently probed her moist warmth. She cried out at the delicious spasms that shuddered through her and she clutched his wrist.

"You want this, don't you, Kat? As much as I do," he murmured huskily. "Show me."

She pressed against his hand, seeking his touch as his fingers slowly stroked deeper. She couldn't hold back a groan of pleasure.

Desire and need and hunger culminated in a joyous release, sending tremors through her. "Mitch!" she cried.

She sagged against his chest, spent and panting, her skin damp. "Mitch..." She sighed, relishing the pulsing aftershocks of passion.

"Ah, Kat," he whispered roughly. "I love to watch you come. You're so wild and free."

"Because of you. You're a fantastic lover, Mitch."

He closed his eyes for a moment and breathed deeply. "Thanks, Kat. I needed to hear that."

She framed his face in her hands. "Oh, Mitch, I want to make you feel as wonderful as I do."

"I hope so," he murmured.

She let her fingers wander slowly over his chest. She nibbled his neck and jaw, then paused for a moment.

"More, Kat. More," he urged.

"Much more," she assured him.

She leaned forward, and the light pressure of her nipples against his chest elicited a gasp of surprise and delight.

She lowered her lips to his. Her tongue invaded his mouth. Then, slowly, she broke the kiss, reluctant to give up her pleasure in it, yet urgent to give him even more. Her fingers and lips worked across his chest, down his belly.

"Kat," he groaned through clenched teeth, "I'm wild with wanting you."

Spurred by his obvious need, she pulled off his slacks and briefs and teased his inner thighs with damp kisses and little nips, feeling his body tense with arousal.

She spread his legs and slipped between them. She ran the end of her tongue up and down the length of his erection. She licked the voluptuous tip, then scored it gently with her teeth, bringing gasps from Mitch.

She moved to mount him.

"No," he begged.

"I want you inside me," she whispered.

"Not now. Not while I'm like this, not while I can only lie here and receive without giving."

She understood his need to participate, to share equally. Wrapping her hand around him, she tugged slowly and gently at first, then gradually increased the pressure and intensity.

His fingers tangled clumsily in the sheets as his body grew rigid with arousal that quickly brought him to climax. He chanted her name like a mantra, "Kat . . . Kat . . . Oh, Kat . . ."

She eased down beside him and kissed his cheek.

"I've wanted this, needed this, for so long." His voice caught. "I had to know. To know if I could function. But I never dared hope making love could be so sensational again."

He paused, then added, "I promised myself not to compare with my memories, but I can't help it."

"Neither can I."

"Well?" he asked, apprehension in his voice.

Her reluctance to admit how deeply his lovemaking had affected her was overridden by the need to tell Mitch the truth to ease his mind. She lifted her head and met his gaze. "This was better, I think."

"Yes," Mitch agreed, then sighed. "It's been a long time."

"A very long time," she said and added silently, *More than three years. For me*, she amended.

"Stay with me tonight, Katharine."

"I'll have to cancel my late date," she teased. "But if you insist . . ."

"I want to sleep with my arms around you."

"Me, too," she admitted. She turned off the light and returned to him, then raised the metal sides of the narrow bed.

"Which one of us are you trying to keep penned in?"

"I'm keeping the world penned out. For tonight." She lowered the head of the bed until the surface was flat.

Cuddled beside him, she remembered the dangers of falling under Mitch's spell. She couldn't risk another night like this. If she let herself get too caught up in a sexual relationship, it might destroy their burgeoning friendship.

With Mitch's arms resting on her, Katharine drifted toward sleep. Suspended between dreaming and wakefulness, she wasn't sure whether she heard Mitch whisper it or if she only dreamed that he had—"Happy Anniversary, love."

8

"DAMMIT! DAMMIT TO HELL!" Mitch shouted as he guided his wheelchair back to his room.

"Take it easy, Mitch," Steve counseled. "Like I told you, recovering from GBS is a marathon, not a sprint. You've plateaued, man. That's all."

Furious, Mitch wouldn't be soothed by platitudes. "Three weeks with no change! How in hell am I supposed to get well if I can't make any progress?"

"Sooner or later, you'll pick up strength again. Meanwhile, you've got to keep working at it."

"I *have* worked at it."

"That's right. You've worked like a madman for the past month. That's why I'm giving you a day off. Think of it as an early Christmas gift."

Mitch sagged against the back of the chair. "And you'd like to be rid of me, wouldn't you?"

"Even Mother Teresa would want to be rid of you when you're in this mood."

If Steve were trapped in this damn chair, he wouldn't be joking, Mitch thought. "Then get out of here. We both need a break."

"See you day after tomorrow, Mitch." His tone softened, "And try not to worry. You've accomplished a lot in a few months."

Mitch snorted derisively.

"If you don't shape up that attitude, I'll take you to a therapy center and show you patients who'll make you feel like a wimp—people who struggle harder than you do against poorer odds of meaningful recovery," Steve said bluntly. "That's a promise, man. Feel sorry for yourself if you want to, but I won't let you enjoy it." He slammed the door as he left.

Mitch cursed and shut his eyes. Ever since he and Katharine had made love the night of their anniversary, he'd been obsessed with his recovery.

That night had demonstrated that he could give her pleasure—and she him. But it wasn't enough—not by a long shot. He wanted to make love to her the way he once had, to plunge deep inside her, driving them both to the brink until they climaxed and lay together amid damp, tangled sheets.

Oh, Katharine had been tactful about it, insisting that what they'd experienced was the best ever, but she'd avoided his bed since that night, repeating her claim that making love with him was risky for her—and pointless. Pointless? Pointless because she didn't love him? Could never love him? Pointless because he was a long way from being the lover she remembered? Pointless because . . . what? He dared not push her for an explanation, fearful of hearing the truth.

Besides, she couldn't—shouldn't—be satisfied with a man as limited as he. If he were stronger, maybe she'd let him be her lover, even though she didn't love him anymore.

Damn! he thought, had he really reached the point of desperation with Kat that he'd settle for so little? No commitment, no love—just sex? He groaned softly. Sex would never be enough—she'd made that clear—and he grudgingly agreed. But if he had any chance to win back her love, he had to regain his ability to demonstrate his love physically.

Tired and depressed, he rang for the nurse and asked her to help him into bed. When the nurse left, Mitch realized he was alone in the house for the first time. The night nurse was no longer needed, Katharine was working late, and the housekeeper had taken a few days' vacation to spend with visiting relatives.

As night closed in, he pressed on the TV with his remote control, needing diversion. He switched from channel to channel, from reruns to sappy Christmas specials. He turned off the set and wished for the thousandth time he could hold a book and read, but turning pages was still beyond his skills. *Damn!*

He studied the bare walls morosely in the lamplight, then lowered his bed, hoping he could sleep off his black mood. With his eyes tightly closed, the silence surrounded him.

He heard the doorbell chime, but the drapes were drawn and he couldn't see out. The door was locked, and he had no way to open it, so he saw no point in calling out to whoever was there. Someone's footsteps descended the stairs.

He heard the kitchen door creak open, then shut. *Katharine?* he wondered. But the footfalls on the hardwood floor were heavier and slower than Katharine's. His heart raced. Someone had broken into the house. And he was helpless! He had no way to defend himself. None at all.

If he called out in challenge, he'd become a target. But if he lay quietly and let someone rob Katharine's house, he'd damn himself forever for his cowardice. *Damn!*

Cold sweat drenched his forehead. He searched for a weapon, something he could raise in defense. Nothing. He elevated his bed so that he sat nearly upright, sucked in a deep breath, and bellowed, *"Who's there?"*

The intruder stalked into the foyer and began sliding apart the doors to his room. Mitch steeled himself to confront the robber, praying that the man was unarmed.

As the door separated, Mitch blanched. Instead of confronting evil incarnate, he faced a short, skinny young man who appeared equally surprised.

"Uh...Mr. Woods? Sorry to disturb you. I'm Jimmy Cochrane, your housekeeper's nephew."

Mitch felt relief sweep through his body as he let out his pent-up breath in a long sigh. "What the hell are you doing here?"

"My aunt forgot a couple of Christmas presents and sent me to get them. She told me not to make a lot of racket because you'd probably be sleeping. I rang the bell because the key she gave me didn't work in the front door, or in the kitchen door, either."

Apprehension knotted Mitch's gut again. "How did you get in?"

"I used a credit card to trip the lock." He grinned proudly. "It was easy."

"A credit card?" Mitch thundered. "You broke in with a lousy credit card?"

Jimmy took several steps backward. "Y-yes, sir. I'm sorry. It seemed okay at the time."

The young man's stricken expression made Mitch realize that he was bellowing at the wrong person. "It's okay, Jim," he said soothingly. "Get what you need and lock up when you leave, for whatever good that'll do."

"Yes, sir. Th-thank you, sir." Jimmy backed from the room and closed the doors.

Katharine was an absolute fool! Mitch thought. Living here without so much as dead-bolt locks to discourage thieves, rapists, murderers. Anyone could break in, overpower her, hurt her, kill her.

She took such risks with her safety and had no one to protect her—least of all her husband. *Husband!* he snorted. What a joke of a husband he was. Loving her made him want to protect her, and he couldn't.

For the first time, Mitch felt his cheeks flush with shame. He was weak. Hell, he was useless; unable to function as Katharine's husband—or lover.

TYPICAL, UNPREDICTABLE Dallas weather, Katharine thought, and decided to serve their simple Christmas Eve meal on the patio so they could savor the warm, sunny weather. After they'd eaten, she brought out a cardboard box. She lifted out a polished wooden briefcase with brass hardware and a leather-wrapped handle and set it on the table in front of Mitch. "Merry Christmas," she said, beaming with pleasure at the admiration in his eyes.

He slid his fingers over the smooth, glossy surface, then awkwardly opened the latch and examined the inside. His voice caught when he tried to speak. "Thank you, Katharine. It's beautiful. You made it, didn't you?"

"Yes. I think every successful businessman needs a personally crafted briefcase, don't you?"

"I do now. Let's go inside and I'll show you my gifts."

Katharine followed his directions and pulled a box from under the secretary's desk. She lifted the lid and was surprised to find a dozen Wedgwood-china-blue place mats—an unlikely gift from a man who took little interest in housewares.

Mitch volunteered proudly, "I made them."

"You did?" Mitch had never made anything for her before. He'd never even bought her a present. When they'd lived in Houston, his secretary had selected gifts for her—expensive and impersonal gifts. She lifted the top mat and examined the even stitches. He'd knitted them on very large needles with thick, smooth cotton yarn. Tears threatened as she envisioned Mitch's struggle for each perfect stitch.

"The occupational therapist chose the color, so I hope you wanted a blue dining room."

She swallowed the lump that filled her throat. "I do now."

"At the rate I'm going, I can knit a whole tablecloth before I get well." He added wryly, "Maybe a couple of bedspreads, a few rugs, some drapes . . .

"But that's not the best part. Look up there, just below the ceiling."

She gazed at a small object that looked like a tiny camera. "What on earth is that?"

"It's part of the security system I had installed."

"You what?"

"I had a security system installed today. The brochures are on the table."

Her voice rose in astonishment. "A security system?"

"Yeah. You have perimeter alarms on the doors and windows, and motion detectors in most of the rooms."

Same old Mitch! she thought, her irritation mounting by the second.

"There's also a 'panic button' by your bed. Push the button and the police are called automatically."

Mitch had the *audacity* to order work done, to bring in people to drill holes in her ceiling—*her* ceiling! Who the hell did he think he was? He acted as if he were the man of the house; as if he were her husband in good standing!

"I don't want to live in a fortress like some paranoid, Mitch. I don't need this stuff. Have it taken out tomorrow," she commanded.

"No." His face was so rigid it could have been cast in stone.

"You're way out of line here, Mitch. This is my house, and I want to do the work on it. I'll get to everything when I have the time—and the money!"

"You'd better learn to protect yourself, Katharine," he shouted.

"And you've decided to be my teacher? What's next, coach? Karate lessons?"

"Oh, hell." His peremptory tone vanished, and his head sagged against the pillow. "You do need security, Katharine," he said patiently. "Someone broke in the other night—with a credit card, for God's sake! You're asking for trouble."

"Someone broke in?" Katharine croaked. "What happened? Why didn't you tell me?"

"It was just the housekeeper's nephew, but he scared the daylights out of me. Someone could get in here and hurt you, Katharine. I can't stand that thought. Keep the system, please—if not for your own safety, then for my peace of mind."

She'd never even thought of Mitch's vulnerability to physical attack. He'd always been so strong he'd seemed invincible. Now he couldn't raise a hand in his own defense. No wonder he was so insistent about safety.

"All right, Mitch," she said reluctantly. "I'll keep the system. But I object to your giving me things that I can't afford to buy on my own. I don't want to owe you anything."

"You don't. It's me who owes you. You've given me so much in the last few months. Time, and care, and a home—more than I can ever repay. A security system isn't even a fair down payment. Don't begrudge what little I can give you."

"Fine. I'll consider it rent. But no more of your old tricks of determining what I need without even consulting me."

WHEN GUS ARRIVED AT NOON to share Christmas dinner with them, Mitch felt apprehensive. The old man had never liked him and had never made a secret of it. But Gus treated him with restrained but genuine courtesy and acceptance. Mitch assumed Gus had mellowed.

After dinner Gus and Katharine exchanged gifts, then Gus excused himself. He returned in a minute with a hand-carved wooden cane, which he laid across Mitch's lap. "It'll be a while before you can use this, boy, but I hear you're doing good on those exercises."

Recognizing Gus's gift as a peace offering of sorts, Mitch felt both grateful and embarrassed. "Thanks, Gus. You're the last person I expected to give me a gift. The cane is perfect." He concentrated on keeping his voice steady. "Having it will make me work harder. I want to be able to use it."

"You will, son." He turned to Katharine. "Is it time to call your folks?"

"Yes. Mitch has volunteered his speaker phone."

Katharine placed the call, and she and Gus sang a rousing chorus of "We Wish You a Merry Christmas" to her parents at their home in Florida.

While Katharine's family caught up on gossip, Mitch watched and felt envious. Even though a thousand miles separated them, the Drakes were still a close-knit, loving family.

What a contrast to his own. His family had been aloof and distant even while his parents were alive. He couldn't imagine a similar telephone call to Francine. As usual, his secretary had selected his sister's gift, so he didn't know what he'd "given" her. He'd received nothing from her. He ought to call her, he thought, but wasn't sure whether she was home or celebrating the holiday on a cruise.

KATHARINE ARRIVED HOME from work on a Thursday evening to find Mitch sullen and brooding. All through January he'd made little progress in his therapy, despite Steve's reassurances.

Tonight he seemed unusually depressed, she thought. "Mitch?"

"You'll want to avoid me tonight. I'm in a rotten mood."

"I know you're disappointed about your recovery progress, but this plateau is only temporary."

"For once, that's not what's eating at me. I— Oh, hell, Katharine. I lost a major customer."

"What happened?"

"Jim and Bob Downing heard that I'm sick, and now they won't do business with Woods, Inc., because they think I'm not strong enough—*competent* enough—to run my company 'in my condition.' They're my biggest customers. I've sold vast amounts of lumber, concrete and Sheetrock plasterboard to their home-construction company for years."

His shoulders sagged against the back of his wheelchair. "I don't know how I'll replace them," he said dispiritedly. "I can't go around the country drumming up business while I'm trapped in this thing." He cursed softly.

Katharine's heart sank. Mitch feared losing the only other thing as important to him as his physical health—Woods, Inc. How could she help? Then a possible solution came to her. "Where is their company located?" she asked.

He sighed wearily. "San Francisco. Why? I sell to them through my Bay Area distribution center."

"Feel like seeing the Golden Gate?"

"Don't joke about this!"

"Is winning back your contract with the Downings worth some extra expense, some risk?"

"Of course, it's worth it. But it's not a matter of just spending money."

"We could do it, Mitch."

"*We?* Do what?"

"Meet with your customers."

"Sure, and convince them I'm a hopeless cripple."

"No! Convince them that you're in charge of the company. You are, you know, and have been since you got out of the ICU. We can show them!"

"But how can you leave your work?"

"I'll ask Gus to take charge tomorrow. He's a good supervisor."

A glimmer of hope lit Mitch's eyes. "What's your plan?"

"We'll fly to San Francisco, then rent a van. We'll find a hotel that's accessible for your chair and meet with your customers there. What do you think?"

"Yeah, maybe we could pull it off. It's worth a try."

Elated at Mitch's agreement, Katharine added, "You call your customers, and I'll make the travel arrangements."

"Can we go tomorrow? The Downings move fast, and I don't want to give them time to find a new supplier."

"We'll make it work."

As she rushed upstairs, Katharine reconsidered her rash decision. Fridays usually were busy because they packed and shipped orders. She ought to be at the plant making sure nothing went awry. They couldn't afford to mix up orders and have to pay for return shipments. Yet Gus assured her he would manage without her.

Then she called Art Harris. His first words were, "I was about to call you! Can you meet early Monday with a group from Invesco?"

Her pulse picked up speed. "Invesco's a major investment firm."

"Specializing in helping small manufacturing companies grow. But they look at deals from a different perspective than most other firms. First, you'll need to break down your projected cash flow by product line rather than lumping all the furniture products together and the playground equipment as another single item."

Katharine stifled a groan. Revising the projections would take many hours. She grabbed a pen and jotted down the topics to be covered. As the list grew longer, she realized she'd need every spare minute between now and Monday to prepare a professional presentation.

When Art hung up, she started thinking about her approach to Invesco. Then she remembered she'd promised to spend tomorrow in San Francisco with Mitch. She'd have to cancel. The future of her own company was at stake. As a businessman, Mitch would understand. After all, he'd asked if she could spare the time.

He'd have to go without her. But who would assist him? Steve could take care of transporting him, but he'd be of little help during the meeting. Perhaps Sam Chandler could meet Mitch in San Francisco. Of course, Sam was unfamiliar with Mitch's limitations, so he wouldn't know how to conceal them. She racked her brain, but came up with no more ideas.

Perhaps they could postpone the meeting until next week. But Mitch believed they needed to act quickly, before the customers found a new supplier.

Mitch needed her, and she needed a chance to show him her own hard-earned business acumen.

She'd have to handle both responsibilities. She'd take along the list of items Art had given her and the raw data she'd base her projections on. There'd be time for work on the plane. Perhaps there'd be lulls in the negotiations with Mitch's customers and she could work on her presentation. Besides, she'd still have the whole weekend to prepare.

ON THEIR LATE-NIGHT flight to San Francisco, Mitch outlined his previous dealings with the Downings, and they mapped out their strategy. At eight o'clock in the morning they checked into the Four Seasons Clift Hotel and put the finishing touches on their scheme. In a small conference room Katharine helped transfer Mitch to a large leather chair, hid the wheelchair in the closet, and laid out copies of the contract his secretary had typed the night before.

The Downings arrived promptly at eight-thirty and shot wary glances at Mitch, gave her the once-over, taking note of her dowdy suit, lack of makeup, ugly glasses, and hair drawn into a tight bun, and shook her hand without enthusiasm.

The brothers were nearly identical, with gray hair, gray suits, gray ties, and gray complexions. Gray personalities, too, she'd bet. Unable to readily distinguish between the men, Katharine mentally dubbed them "the Jim-Bobs." With effort, she smothered the smile and stopped the conspiratorial wink she wished to flash in Mitch's direction.

When everyone else was seated, Mitch began the meeting, firmly establishing his authority. "Jim, Bob, I appreciate your making yourselves available on short notice. Ms. Drake, will you take notes on any points that require additional negotiation? As always, I'd like your input on those matters."

Good move, Mitch, she thought. He made his health a nonissue from the start, conducting the meeting with an air of business-as-usual.

The Jim-Bobs stuck to contract matters, as well. Throughout the morning they discussed quantities of cement in tons, lumber in thousands of board feet, and pipe in diameters. At first, the Jim-Bobs were reluctant to accept the terms Mitch offered. Their reservations were not a negotiating technique, she soon realized. The brothers were still skeptical about the state of Mitch's health . . . and his company.

Mitch kept the pressure on, offering various proposals, hoping to wear down their resistance. Gradually the discussion turned to delivery dates and penalties for noncompliance. Without saying so, the Downings had acquiesced and turned to the details of the sales.

When the Jim-Bobs objected to one of the terms, Mitch turned to Katharine and asked, "Ms. Drake, do you think we can deliver that much Sheetrock in three months?"

She had no idea, but offered confidently, "It will be tough, Mr. Woods, but for customers like these... Let's agree to the shortened delivery date, but cut our penalty in half if we fail to deliver. After all, they're asking a lot."

Mitch's eyes widened at her bold proposal. "Good suggestion, Ms. Drake. What do you say, gentlemen?"

The Downings pursed their lips, glanced at each other, and nodded.

Katharine pretended to study her notes to conceal her grin.

At noon one of the Downings suggested they order from room service and continue the meeting.

"If you don't mind, Bob, Ms. Drake and I need to confer on some separate matters. I suggest we take a break and reconvene in an hour."

The men agreed and left. As the door closed behind them, Mitch sighed with relief. "I thought for a minute I was doomed to struggle with a grilled-cheese sandwich—a dead giveaway."

Slowly he raised his forearms from the table. "Would you rub my arms, Katharine? They're numb from four hours of inactivity."

As Katharine massaged his muscles through the sleeves of his shirt and jacket, he added, "You're one hell of a negotiator, lady. 'Let's cut the penalty in half,'" he mimicked. "I was willing to give them what they asked for."

"In dealing with vendors and buyers in my business, I've learned that audacity sometimes pays."

He chuckled with obvious pleasure. "I ought to put you on the payroll. You've earned a year's pay this morning."

"It's good to know I can get a job if I ever need one, but I'm not interested." Obviously he regarded her work as a hobby. That much hadn't changed in the past five months. She contained her annoyance and ordered lunch.

During the afternoon session, the phone rang. Conveniently seated beside it, Katharine turned on the speaker phone. "Mitch," Sam Chandler said, "I just got a call. The Wysocki deal is back on. Can you stay over and meet with their people this weekend?"

Mitch raised his eyebrows at Katharine. "How about it, Ms. Drake? Can you stay over?"

With no clue about the Wysocki deal, Katharine pretended to examine her calendar. She had planned on getting home tonight so she could prepare for the Invesco meeting.

Mitch watched her intently. "I'd like to get that one wrapped up, Ms. Drake," he urged.

Perhaps Mitch wouldn't need her to cover for him on the Wysocki deal, and she'd have time for her own work. "Sure, I can stay tomorrow if you can."

"Okay, Sam. Please fax us the papers this afternoon."

Katharine gave Sam the hotel's fax number and disconnected the call.

"We'll have to work late tonight, Ms. Drake, to be ready in the morning."

Katharine smiled with more confidence than she felt. "No problem, sir."

By midafternoon they'd worked out all the terms of the Downings' contract, and Katharine called Mitch's secretary who typed the revisions and faxed a completed copy back to them. One of the Downings signed two copies and shoved the contracts across the table to Mitch.

Katharine stopped breathing. Mitch couldn't pick up the slender pen, much less sign his name. *Damn!*

Mitch caught her gaze. "Ms. Drake, you put this deal together. You ought to sign it in your capacity as vice president of Woods, Inc."

As she picked up the contract, Katharine hoped her broad smile showed pleasure, not relief. "Why, thank you, Mr. Woods. This gesture means a lot to me." She scribbled her name on each copy and handed one to a Jim-Bob. "It's been a pleasure, gentlemen."

One of the gray men said, "This calls for a drink. Shall we head for the bar?"

Mitch hesitated. "Ms. Drake and I need to get started on the Wysocki deal . . ."

Flushed with their success, Katharine interrupted. "We have to make some phone calls, but after that, I'd like to take a short break, Mr. Woods." She saw doubt in his eyes. "It'll be all right," she added firmly.

"Okay. Give us an hour and we'll meet you in the Redwood Room."

When the door closed, Katharine said, "I'm not authorized to sign for your company, Mitch. The contract isn't valid."

"No problem. I'm the only director, so I'll have Sam draw up a resolution electing you a vice president, effective yesterday. He's authorized to sign company documents for me, so everything will be legal."

Amused by her new title, Katharine checked the hall to be sure the Jim-Bobs were gone. She helped transfer Mitch to his wheelchair, and they headed for the elevator, giggling like schoolchildren who've tricked their teacher.

When the elevator doors closed behind them, Katharine pressed the button for their floor and bent to kiss Mitch's cheek.

"Sit in my lap and give me a real kiss, woman," he growled.

Katharine complied, wrapping her arms around his neck. Their kiss began as a celebration of victory, but quickly escalated to hungry passion. When the elevator stopped, Katharine reached behind her and pushed another button.

She was barely aware that the doors slid open again until she heard a collective gasp. She broke the kiss and looked over her shoulder at a group of people waiting for the elevator. She smiled wickedly, pushed their floor button and the doors closed to the sound of applause from the spectators.

"I'm sorry," Mitch murmured as he nibbled at her lips.

"Umm?"

"That we're not in the Bank of America building."

"Umm?"

"More floors." He deepened the kiss, drawing her closer against his chest until the elevator stopped at their floor.

He guided the chair to his door and waited while Katharine, still sitting in his lap, unlocked the door. He drove into the room, stopped, and captured her mouth with his. Heat and desire built to a fever pitch, leaving each gasping for breath.

He nuzzled her neck. "God, Kat, I want you. Cancel out with the Downings, and we'll make love."

Reluctantly, Katharine climbed off his lap. "You're hesitant to have a drink with them because you don't want them to find out your true condition, aren't you?"

"That's *one* of the reasons," he admitted with a lecherous grin.

"Does it matter, now that they were impressed enough to sign a big contract?"

"Probably not, but fooling them was the whole point."

Katharine couldn't hold back a devilish smile.

"What are you thinking, Kat?"

"They're impressed with your business prowess. I think we can impress them in other ways. We'll get you ready, then you can go downstairs alone while I prepare a little surprise."

"Kat?" he asked uncertainly.

"Don't worry, you'll love it. And it'll blow the Jim-Bobs out of their gray socks."

Mitch laughed at her characterization and capitulated. She shaved away his day's growth of beard, helped him change into a sport shirt, kissed him quickly, then left.

MITCH GUIDED HIS CHAIR to the bar. Two stories high and paneled with redwood, he'd always thought it a most intimate place for a drink. Tonight he and Katharine would share it with the Downing brothers. What a waste.

He paused in the doorway, located his hosts, and headed toward their table. Both men arched their brows as he approached, obviously surprised at this evidence of incapacity. "Gentlemen, I hope I haven't kept you waiting," Mitch said, ignoring their stares.

When a cocktail waitress approached, he ordered a gin and tonic with a straw. The Downings watched him closely. Lord, he thought, Katharine and her surprise had better get here in a hurry. He couldn't stand much more of their silent inquisition.

When the waitress placed his drink on the table, he brought his chair closer and sipped from the straw. "My compliments to the bartender. He's got a way with lime." He knew he was babbling, but felt compelled to fill the silence without acknowledging the curiosity writ large on the Downings' faces. *Hurry, Katharine!* he urged silently.

He heard a slight stir, turned to the doorway, and choked on his drink. Katharine stood under a dim spotlight, her hair a red-gold aura around her face and shoulders. She spotted him, flashed a dazzling smile and strode confidently toward him in a green dress that clung to every curve. Reminded of the night they'd met, and all its implications, he felt his body quicken.

He gauged the Downings' reaction. Two sets of gray eyes bulged from faces reddened with shock. They lurched to their feet as she drew near. "Ms. Drake?" Jim asked in a high-pitched quaver.

"How nice to see you again," Bob completed lamely, as he fumbled to seat her before he collapsed into his own chair.

"I hope I haven't kept you gentlemen waiting," she apologized.

Both men shook their heads, their gazes fastened on one of the thin straps of her gown as it slipped toward the edge of her shoulder.

Thoroughly enjoying the men's amazement, Mitch turned to Katharine. "What would you like to drink, my dear?"

Katharine licked her lips as she considered her choice. Her smoldering gaze held his as she spoke. "I'll have a Chambord Royale liqueur, please."

She sipped the raspberry drink, occasionally licking away traces from her lips.

Mitch managed to glance at the Downings, pleased that their eyes were riveted on Katharine.

Wild with the need to touch her, hold her, love her, Mitch cleared his throat. "When you finish your drink, we need to give the Wysocki deal our attention, Kat," he told her, grateful that his voice sounded assured.

She gave the Downings an electrifying smile and said throatily, "Mitch is a demanding taskmaster, but he's taught me *so-o-o* much."

As she stood, Mitch wondered what the speed record was for motorized wheelchairs, certain that he could break it.

9

As soon as they were inside his room, Mitch reached for Katharine's hand, but she stepped back and teasingly asked, "Whatever do you have in mind, sir?"

His heart hammered as Katharine languorously raised her fingers and fanned out her coppery hair, then let the strands fall to her shoulders. Slowly she glided her hands down the front of her shimmery green dress. She outlined her breasts seductively, her chest rising and falling with each shallow breath.

"You know damn well what I want," Mitch rasped. "Unless I miss my guess, you want it, too."

"*Moi?*" she inquired, pouting.

"Don't toy with me, you temptress! I swear, Kat, if you don't come to me, I'll lunge out of this chair, drag you to the floor, and take you. I think I could do it right now. This second."

"As I recall, you like making love on carpets." She approached him slowly, hooking a finger beneath a wayward strap and nudging it off her shoulder. The emerald fabric slipped precariously low over the pale mound of her breast.

Katharine eased into his lap and wrapped her arms around his neck. She brushed her lips across his, then opened her mouth eagerly as his tongue probed the delicate recesses. When he lifted his head to drag in a much-needed breath, she unbuttoned his shirt and dropped damp little kisses on his chest, heating up his skin and his desire.

Again she covered his lips with hers, this time plunging her tongue into his mouth. Mitch groaned with urgency. Slowly, he raised his hand to her silk-covered breasts, wishing he could skim his fingers lightly over the fabric and make her flesh quiver with desire as he'd once been able to do so easily. Instead, he cupped one breast in his palm and teased her nipple with the pad of his thumb, loving the sensation of soft silk over her heated flesh.

She arched her back, giving him fuller access. "Good...so good." She tugged at her dress, baring her breast.

Emboldened by her response, he dipped his head and took the swollen peak into his mouth, suckling gently. She whispered his name and buried her fingers in his hair, clutching him against her.

He brought a hand to her other breast, caressing it, though cursing inwardly at the awkwardness of his fingers. Katharine seemed unaware of his clumsiness, for she writhed in his lap and moaned softly.

"You're overdressed, Kat," he murmured.

She got up, letting the dress fall in an emerald pool around her feet, and stood before him, gloriously naked. Moving closer, she slid her knees on either side of his thighs so that she knelt in his chair.

His tongue dipped into her navel, darting in and out, then circling. Breathing raggedly, she gripped his shoulders to steady herself.

He trailed kisses down her taut belly, making her flesh quiver. She arched toward him, encouraging his exploration. He gazed at her, savoring the sight of her so aroused by him—her eyes closed, head thrown back.

"More, love?" he crooned, wanting to satisfy their raging needs. He lifted his arms and stiffly stroked her back.

Her breath caressing his ear, she whispered, "You're overdressed, Mitch."

She slid her palms over his chest, teasing his nipples, first with her fingertips, then with her tongue. Slowly she pushed his shirt down his arms. He wanted to rush her, but she seemed bent on taking her time, teasing him, prolonging and building the pleasure that pulsed through him.

When she finally discarded his shirt, she smiled wantonly and inquired, "Bed or carpet?"

"Bed," he answered, certain that when he finished making love to her he'd be too exhausted to move again.

With the transfer board, she helped him onto the bed and removed the rest of his clothing. Then he reached for her, wanting to pleasure her.

"No," she murmured. "It's your turn." And she began stroking, kissing, teasing his body.

When he could stand no more, he pleaded, "Take me inside you, Kat."

He watched heightened desire flare in her eyes as she straddled him and slowly lowered herself onto his throbbing erection. His breath a shallow hiss, he arched his back to drive deeper inside her, and heard her gasp of surprise and pleasure at his regained strength.

She set the pace and gradually they accelerated their movements until he exploded with release deep within her. Moments later she tensed as she climaxed, then collapsed beside him.

They lay together, panting, touching, kissing, loving—both caught in a swirl of emotions. It was several minutes before Katharine lifted her head and smiled, with kiss-swollen lips. "Was that okay?"

"Off the top of the chart."

Katharine snuggled beside him, one leg draped across his, her fingers idly stroking his chest. As he drifted toward sleep, a thought suddenly occurred to him. How could he have been so stupid?

"Katharine? Oh, God, Katharine. I'm sorry. I should have thought—"

"About what?" Katharine asked.

"Protecting us! I didn't think . . . I mean, I had something, but . . ."

Katharine lay her fingertips across his mouth. "Shh. You needn't worry. I'm on the Pill."

She sat up and seemed to consider her next words. "I visited my gynecologist the day after Francine conned me into bringing you to my house. I wanted you every time I was with you, and I knew my resistance would eventually crumble. It was just a matter of time." She eased off the bed. "I'm going to take a shower," she said firmly.

Mitch listened to the sound of the spray and pictured Katharine with rivulets of water coursing down her warm, rosy skin. He knew that he loved her, and that lovemaking was only a small but *vital* part of what he wanted to share with her in the future.

Yet he feared that Katharine seemed unable to love him the way he loved her. She took their overpowering desire for each other for granted. He understood; he'd been the same way, once. After she'd left him, he'd been involved with two attractive women, both of them petite, pretty redheads. Like Katharine. So he'd had two brief affairs, each of them an ultimate disappointment because they'd lacked passion—the emotion he'd shared so totally with Katharine. When the second affair ended, he'd finally admitted that only with Katharine could he have the love—the intimacy, passion and commitment—he craved.

Katharine's words tonight anguished him. He'd believed they'd become lovers and best friends. He'd tried to show her his love, his respect, his caring. But apparently she still thought they shared only sex.

He'd have the weekend to prove to her that they could build a new, lasting relationship. He was a different man, a better man, than he'd been three years ago. He'd win her over, by God.

KATHARINE FINISHED HER shower and donned her robe. "It's late, Mitch," she said, adopting a businesslike tone. "We'd better start on the Wysocki deal."

"There is no Wysocki deal." He ducked his head, seeming embarrassed. "I arranged for Sam to call us so you'd spend the weekend with me away from our daily routines."

"What?" she demanded.

"I planned a romantic getaway for us."

"Without consulting me?" Her voice rose, sounding shrill in her own ears.

"It was a surprise."

"There you go again! You make plans for me without bothering to discuss them first. Damn it, Mitch. Who do you think you are?"

"I'm sorry, Katharine. I thought you'd be pleased to have a little time away from work."

"I'd love to get away, but I have responsibilities. I need to spend every spare minute preparing for a meeting on Monday. Did it occur to you that I'd have other plans?"

"Then we'll go home," he said calmly. "Maybe we'll have another chance."

She had only to say *yes*, but the word wouldn't come from her mouth. She did want time alone with Mitch, and tomorrow might be her only chance.

"No, you're right. I could use a change of scenery. What if we stay until tomorrow evening? I can work tonight and all day Sunday."

"Would you stay longer if I helped you prepare for your meeting?"

But Mitch must never know of how precarious her financial condition was! Recalling their arguments over her art-supply store, she feared a replay. Or he might offer her money again, perhaps calling it compensation for her help with the Downings. But she'd fought too hard for her independence to surrender it to him again by taking his money.

"Thanks, Mitch, but this planning is a one-woman job. Besides, you're probably exhausted. It's been a long, hectic day for you."

"You're right." He sighed in disappointment. "Some of it was especially 'hectic' for a man who's out of practice. Good night, Kat. Don't stay up too late."

AT FOUR O'CLOCK in the morning, Katharine stretched and yawned. Her work had progressed slowly because thoughts of Mitch preoccupied her. The healthier he got, the more he reverted to the old Mitch, as she had supposed he would.

Making love with him again had been a foolish risk. She'd kidded herself when she vowed she could make love with him and accept that they were on a dead-end road. In a few weeks—months if she was lucky—he'd return to Houston and pick up his life. Despair swept over her. So little time remained for them to be together.

She hated the prospect of losing Mitch. But, then again, he'd never been hers to lose. He'd always lived his own life, focused on his own interests. She'd been only a peripheral part of his life, yet she'd been dominated by him. She'd come too far, become too self-reliant, to ever play the subservient little woman again. And, of course, he didn't want her back.

Confused by her emotions, Katharine acknowledged that continuing to make love with Mitch would be foolhardy. It would only make her more certain of her love for him; would only make it harder to accept the truth—that they couldn't live together and be happy.

She slid into bed beside him. At least they'd have a day in San Francisco. She wanted a memory that would last a lifetime.

"HAVE YOU EXPLORED THE Pacific Coast and Wine Country?" Mitch asked Katharine early the next morning.

"No, but I hear it's lovely." Her spirits rose. Mitch had planned a romantic day. At least she *hoped* romance was his intent. What if he'd scheduled tours of wineries, plus a lecture on barrel staves? "What do you have in mind?"

He fixed her with a mock leer.

"I meant, what other activities do you have planned?"

"Nothing. I just thought of it this morning. We'll spend the weekend and check out some fabulous scenery, eat some fabulous food, make some extremely fabulous love."

"You really didn't have a schedule, make reservations?"

"No."

The old Mitch rarely acted spontaneously, she thought. Nor did he plan romantic weekends. Perhaps there was hope, after all.

But the whole weekend? She shoved aside her doubts. "Perfect."

KATHARINE SETTLED MITCH and his chair in the van, and they drove across Golden Gate Bridge under a bright, clear sky. He directed her to the Pacific Coast Highway. Captivated by the rugged beauty of the coast,

Katharine parked at a viewing point and lowered Mitch from the van. They held hands near the edge of the cliff and gazed down at the pounding surf.

After the second stop, Mitch seemed impatient.

"Don't make any more stops," he said. "There's something else I want to show you."

Mitch directed her onto a secondary road. "There it is!" he said excitedly.

She stopped in the parking area and looked toward the imposing stone building that housed Korbel Champagne Cellars, situated amid flower gardens and surrounded by massive redwoods. She could barely contain her delight at the glorious sight.

"Oh, Mitch, how lovely! Can we tour it?"

"Sure." She saw pleasure in his face.

But as they crossed the parking lot for a closer view of the cellars and adjacent gardens, Katharine realized that access would be difficult for Mitch.

As if he'd read her mind, he suggested, "You take the tour, Kat. I'll wait for you, then we'll find something for lunch."

Wandering through the winery with a group of strangers held little appeal for her. "I've lived for almost twenty-nine years without knowing how champagne is made. I can last a while longer. Now, about lunch—"

"There's a little shop. Let's pick up a snack."

They sat at a picnic table surrounded by redwood trees. She cut fruit and cheese into thick slices so Mitch could handle them, and they shared a glass of champagne.

"Fabulous scenery, fabulous food," Katharine murmured. "Now, what was the third item?"

"Let's hit the road," he suggested, his voice lacking the warmth of hers.

"Are you tired, Mitch? We can go back to San Francisco or find somewhere close by and rest."

"I'm not tired," he protested. "Let's keep going."

She settled him and his chair in the van, and they drove farther north along the coast. Late in the afternoon they found a quaint inn overlooking the Pacific, but were daunted by its steep stairs. Katharine sighed in anticipation. The porch would be a perfect place to watch the sunset.

Definitely romantic, she thought. She checked with the owner and learned he had a room available and that they could come around the back where there were only two steps. She lowered Mitch from the van and helped push his chair over the ground. With the owner's help, she lifted the chair up the steps and onto the porch, already envisioning sharing the sunset with Mitch.

He guided his chair to the bedroom door the owner pointed to, stopped, and muttered, "Damn! It's too narrow!"

Dismayed, Katharine asked if there were other downstairs bedrooms. She hid her disappointment when she learned there weren't. "Would it be all right if we watched the sunset from your porch?" she asked with enthusiasm.

"Why sure, lady. Sorry about the door. When you get ready to leave, give me a holler and I'll help you with that—"

"I don't want to stay," Mitch grumbled. "Let's go now."

Unsettled by his restiveness, Katharine stopped at several other Victorian bed-and-breakfasts, but none was wheelchair-accessible. Finally she gave up and checked them into an inexpensive motel whose only attributes were wide doors and no stairs.

Mitch surveyed the room, obviously disgusted. "Yeah. This is exactly what I had in mind. Something furnished in Early Tacky and lacking amenities such as a view and room service."

Katharine helped transfer him to the bed. The mattress was much too soft, robbing Mitch of most of his ability to move.

"Perfect." He punctuated his word with a curse.

Katharine pretended to test the mattress. "Umm. Not quite perfect. But I'll bet we can 'make some extremely fabulous love' on it. First, though, how about a bath, Mitch?"

"Yeah. Okay," he agreed dully.

Katharine decided to make it a memorable bath. Working slowly, she removed his clothes with caressing hands. She filled the ice bucket with warm water, then scented it with a few drops of Mitch's woodsy after-shave.

She washed his back, stroking his skin with a soapy cloth, then removing the soap with a fresh cloth, designing each touch to stimulate him.

She lavished attention on his buttocks and long legs and carefully washed each toe. Returning to his shoulders and back, she kneaded the tight muscles there, eliciting a contented sigh from Mitch. Soon she felt his tension ease.

When she helped him turn over to finish his bath, she noted with pleasure that he was already aroused.

"Kat." The husky timbre of his voice made her skin tingle. "If you don't stop this in three days, I'll whisper for help."

"I'll beat the deadline," she promised. "But just barely." When at last she'd finished bathing him, she tossed the towel aside, kicked off her shoes, and slid onto the bed beside him.

Desire flamed in his eyes. She nipped at his mouth until he parted his lips, which she traced with her tongue. Then she pulled away and quickly shed her clothes. Returning eagerly to Mitch, she caressed his shoulders, his chest, his thighs.

As their passion mounted, she joined their bodies and felt desperate urgency in his thrusts, as though something besides desire drove him. After reaching a shattering, bittersweet climax, they lay together.

Overwhelmed by the intensity of her love for him, Katharine ran her hands over his body again, memorizing the feel of his taut muscles.

"I'm so sorry some things frustrated you today. There are so many unknowns that sometimes you want to give up. But no matter what happens, Mitch," she said, her voice breaking, "I love you."

Shock registered in his eyes. "Katharine, I . . . I don't want your pity."

Pity! Good Lord! How could he reject her love so callously? Regard her feelings for him as pity? She'd never pitied him—not even when he hovered near death. It seemed that all these months she'd fooled herself—she'd let herself believe that he cared for her; let herself hope that he'd grown to love her.

How foolish she'd been to think Mitch had changed and had revised his opinion of her. He clearly believed she was so shallow that what she felt was pity, not love; and he was so absorbed in his own problems that he'd ignored the new intimacy that had blossomed between them. She felt empty, bereft of even a shred of hope.

"You're wallowing in *self*-pity, Mitch," she said. "You're just too blind to see it."

"I'm sorry, Katharine. I don't want to hurt you. But it just isn't working between us."

"It's okay." Tears burned her eyes. She lowered her head and blinked away the evidence of her pain, then rolled over to the far side of the spongy mattress. She clung to the edge, resisting gravity's attempt to drag her down the slope created by Mitch's greater weight. She needed desperately to be alone, but the far side of the mattress was the best she could do at the moment.

When she was sure he was asleep, she locked herself in the bathroom and wept.

10

MITCH RECLINED IN HIS seat on the flight to Dallas. He'd scored a personal victory over GBS with this business coup. He ought to feel proud of himself, confident of his physical recovery and his professional prowess. But Katharine deserved the credit for both victories. He'd just been along for the ride.

Katharine. He'd been a fool to think he could win her love. Hell, he was crippled and would be for a long time—maybe forever. Over the past few months he'd been stupid as well as crippled; his stubborn pride had blocked reality from him, and his money had bought him insulation, not freedom.

He'd been so damn naive to think he was mobile. At Katharine's house he had a swarm of attendants who were so efficient that he forgot how dependent he really was.

Alone and away with Katharine, he'd been forced to face his limitations because of the obstacles surrounding him. She helped him with his food. She loaded and unloaded him into the van. She'd missed a sunset and the tour of a winery because he was crippled and she wouldn't leave him. She bathed him—oh, Lord, did she bathe him.

It was time he faced the reality of his dependency like a man. He couldn't keep Katharine shackled to him any longer. He loved her too much to sentence her to a life of ministering to him.

Staring vacantly out of the plane's window, he recalled Katharine's words. "I love you, Mitch." A few days ago when he was still living in his fantasy world, he'd have sold his soul to hear those words. By Saturday night it was too late, for he knew the truth.

This trip had proved how much he'd deluded himself. He was a long way from being whole again, from being worthy of Katharine. He cringed at the truth: He might *never* be worthy of her.

By damn, the least he could do was salvage his honor. He'd give Katharine her freedom. That was all she'd ever wanted, and she deserved to be truly free. He'd get out of her life. He'd deny his own needs, no matter the cost. Losing Kat would break his heart, he knew, but he refused to dwell on that now.

He glanced across the narrow aisle at Katharine as she reviewed papers and worked her calculator, acting as though he'd ceased to exist. With clumsy fingers he brushed at the tears of frustration welling in his eyes.

Someday you'll thank me, love, he promised silently.

"GOOD MORNING!" Katharine greeted the Invesco representatives with forced enthusiasm. She shook hands all around, then took a seat in their small conference room, grateful that her puffy eyes and sallow skin complemented her contrived unattractiveness. She'd been up all night preparing the presentation. Even so, it was far from her best work, but the best she could do, given the limited amount of time she'd had.

She accepted a cup of coffee—her third of the day—and it was only eight o'clock.

"Let's get started, Ms. Drake," one of them instructed.

Katharine began her presentation by describing the company's history and her plans for its future. She straightened her posture and forced herself to sound authoritative. "To carry out my plans, I require an innovative investor, a company willing to nurture potential."

As she talked, she watched their faces. The woman who led the team seemed sympathetic. Perhaps she'd be more inclined than the men to invest in a woman's business.

Buoyed by that slender hope, Katharine continued brightly. "I'm here to demonstrate that my company has potential. If you'll look at the data behind tab four, I think you'll agree that with a cash infusion, I can begin producing the playground equipment at a reasonable price."

The Invesco team members listened politely to her recitation, asking no questions. Katharine recognized their lack of interest as they idly thumbed through the pages of the business plan. One man glanced at his watch every few minutes, then frowned, clearly wishing he were somewhere else.

She racked her brain for a hook—something to grab and hold their attention. When nothing came to mind, she gave up and said, "That completes my presentation. Do you have any questions?" Her voice had become a tired, dispirited rasp in her own ears.

"Thank you, Ms. Drake. Perhaps we'll be in touch," the woman said.

The cool don't-call-us-we'll-call-you statement drove home her failure to sell them on her company. She wondered again if two days' more preparation could have changed the result. Would they have been more receptive if she'd been well rested, alert and cheerful?

"Fool," she uttered under her breath as she and Art Harris left the meeting.

Art put his hand on her arm. "Yes, they're fools if they pass up this investment. Come on, I'll walk you to the elevator and we can talk about other possibilities."

Katharine trudged along beside him.

"I know you're disappointed, Katharine, but we'll keep looking. There are investors out there who will see your company's potential." Art spoke with renewed confidence. "All we have to do is find them. That's my job, and I'll do it."

"Please do it fast. I'm running out of time." In about two months she'd have to begin laying off employees, and it made business sense to start with the student part-timers. Given a choice, she'd rather fire herself.

"I know time is short," Art assured her. "Frankly, it's taken longer than I expected. Fortunately, you've done a great job of stretching your resources. Hold on for as long as you can. I promise you I'll redouble my effort to find the right firm."

FEBRUARY ALWAYS SEEMED the longest month to Katharine. Amid the bitter cold weather, Dallas twice was brought to a standstill when ice storms transformed the streets into treacherous skating rinks. Even on better days, the sky looked leaden, threatening.

For the first time, she hated going to the plant every day, hated to work until late at night. Yet every day she dragged through her routine like a robot. Depressing as it was to contemplate the future prospects of The KD Line, work at least kept her out of the house, away from Mitch.

Most nights when she arrived home, he was still awake, but was either engrossed in business matters or working with weights to strengthen his arms and legs. He seemed obsessed with his therapy again.

One evening he called to her as she entered the foyer. "Katharine! Come see my new toy."

Puzzled by his excitement, she opened the door.

Mitch patted the wheels of his new chair. "Look. No motor! This baby's Mitch-powered!"

"You're making progress these days," she said, hoping her feeble smile conveyed enthusiasm.

"Yeah," he agreed. "I've decided to get my act together and finish therapy as fast as I can."

"That's good." She ought to be more pleased with this evidence of his recovery, she thought sourly, because each bit of progress brought him closer to freedom. But he was driven toward his goal by pride—the same pride that blinded him to her love.

THE FOLLOWING SATURDAY afternoon, Mitch roamed the lower floor of the house practicing in his new wheelchair. He stopped Katharine as she headed for the utility room.

"If you have time, I'd like to get out of the house for a while."

He looked so bored that Katharine felt duty-bound to agree. "Where do you want to go?"

"Anywhere. Just out."

"How about a mall? You can maneuver your new toy to your heart's content." She tried halfheartedly for a cheerful tone, and missed.

"Good."

She loaded him into the van. As she drove to Town East Mall, they remained silent; the atmosphere was uncomfortably tense.

While Mitch wheeled himself through the crowd, she lagged behind, pretending to browse. As had become their practice, they were together, yet each was alone. She thought of how much fun they would have had a few weeks ago. They'd have laughed together at window displays, shared private jokes, and returned home tired but exhilarated.

Today they remained quiet and withdrawn—Mitch's lackluster thank-you breaking the silence when she helped push his chair up the ramp to her front door.

THE NEXT SATURDAY, Mitch was elated that a friend from Houston came to spend the evening with him. After Mitch briefed him on his battle with GBS, Josh asked, "What about Kathie? I guess you've worked things out?"

Mitch wanted to talk about anything but Katharine. His emotions ran so strong, he feared he'd reveal too much. "No. We haven't worked anything out. And we won't." He shrugged. "It's probably for the best." He hoped he sounded philosophical rather than defeated.

"Let's get out of here, man. Go clubbing—" Josh's glance swept the wheelchair "—or whatever you're ready for."

"Clubbing sounds goods." *It sounds better than sitting here and talking about Katharine*, he reflected.

After several tries, Josh managed to load him into the van and drove to a club filled with smoke and loud music.

Parked at a table, Mitch surveyed his surroundings and forced a smile. "Great idea, Josh. I need a break like this," he lied. He'd spent little time in bars since his undergraduate days. Not much had changed.

Drink in hand, Josh wandered off to flirt and dance. After a while, he brought a dancing partner to the table, introduced her to Mitch, and then returned to the dance floor.

Mitch bought the young woman a drink and half listened to her monologue about her boring job. He had several more drinks to tune her out. Apparently she gave up on him, because she soon excused herself and disappeared into the crowd.

The thick smoke made Mitch's eyes water, and his head pounded in time with the bass drum. He drank several more rounds to dull his senses. *I'm drunk on my ass*, he thought suddenly. *What the hell! I've earned it.* He ordered another round and finished it before Josh found him slumped in his chair.

Fortunately, Josh, a moderate drinker, drove them to Katharine's house and pushed Mitch up the ramp and into his room. He tried to lift Mitch onto his bed, but Mitch dimly realized he was little more than dead weight. Mitch tried to explain the use of the transfer board, but he was unable to form a coherent sentence. The two men shouted at each other, struggling to reposition Mitch's uncooperative limbs.

In a few minutes Katharine appeared in a robe. "Uh-oh," Mitch stage-whispered to Josh. "She's ma-a-ad. We've been bad, Josh." He tried to wink, but both lids dropped. He decided to keep them closed to avoid facing Katharine's anger.

Without a word, Katharine produced the transfer board. With Josh's help, she dumped Mitch onto his bed.

Well, hell, this is a new low, he thought. And Katharine had witnessed it. It shouldn't matter now, but he hated for her to see him foolishly out of control. "This is your fault," he muttered. "All your fault."

In the morning, when he was sober, he'd figure out why.

SEVERAL NIGHTS LATER, Katharine passed by Mitch's open door and saw him sitting up in his bed, lifting small dumbbells over his head.

"How's it going?"

"Good," he said diffidently. "Steve said I should use a regular bed. I'm strong enough to get into the chair by myself now."

"Congratulations."

"Do you want to build the bed?"

Build something else for him? she thought. Oh, sure, she'd gladly tear out her heart making another love offering to go with the chess set and the briefcase. She'd make him a sumptuous bed as a gift. Then she'd ice-skate in hell.

She fought for a restrained tone. "Why would I want to do that?"

"You make so many things for your house, I thought you might want to make the beds." He chuckled. "Literally."

Somewhat mollified, Katharine felt her anger recede. After all, he was regaining his strength. She guessed for his health's sake that his self-absorption was beneficial.

"I'm sorry. I really don't have time. And the beds that came with the house are old and nearly worn-out."

She ought to offer to take him shopping, but the thought of helping him into and out of the van, the thought of touching him, of spending several cozy hours alone with him, depressed her.

"I'll have a new one delivered tomorrow," she said.

"No. I'll make the arrangements."

"In that case, select what you want, pay for it, and take it with you when you leave."

"If that's what you want."

"Then it's settled." Katharine turned to leave.

"Katharine?" Mitch's tone of voice suddenly sounded urgent.

She froze.

"I appreciate your friendship...more than you'll ever know."

"You're welcome," she managed to mutter. "Good night."

"Yeah," he grunted. "Good night."

On the way to her bedroom, she cursed her stupidity for the thousandth time. She wished she had a friend, a confidant, someone to tell her troubles to, someone to help her deal with the pain. But she couldn't burden Gus with both her business worries and her private misery. Talking with her parents by phone was so distant and wouldn't give her the comfort she hungered for. And she'd seen few of her friends since Mitch had reentered her life. Another blunder, she acknowledged. But there was the bitter consolation that at the rate Mitch was recovering, he'd be gone soon, and she'd start rebuilding her life for the second time.

MARCH BROUGHT WARMER weather and the promise of an early spring. On a sunny Saturday morning, Katharine stood in the kitchen, mixing paint for one of the bedrooms. She'd quit working on the dining room after they returned from San Francisco, concentrating instead on rooms where she wouldn't see or hear Mitch.

She'd almost got the color she wanted when she heard Mitch's wheelchair in the hall. For a moment she thought about rushing up the back stairs to avoid him.

No, dammit, she thought, this was *her* house. She refused to hide from anyone. Pleased with her resolution, she smiled when he wheeled into the kitchen.

He stared out the window into the backyard as though fascinated by the three scraggly bushes, the dead lawn, and the crumbling brick patio. After a moment he asked, "Is there any coffee left?"

"It's old, but it's hot." She poured a cup and set it on the table where he could reach it easily.

When he lifted the big mug by its handle and raised it to his mouth with little effort, Katharine recognized the major improvement in his motor skills, but made no comment.

Silence stretched between them. After a few minutes, Katharine turned to the paint can and stirred absently.

She heard Mitch draw a deep breath.

"Katharine?" he said, his voice flat.

She faced him only to discover that he was staring out the window again. He cleared his throat and caught her gaze for a moment, then studied the wall behind her.

"I'm coming to the end of my therapy. I'll be leaving soon."

She nodded, waiting for him to continue.

"We ought to tie up the loose ends in our lives."

"Yes." She struggled to keep her voice even. "It's time, I guess."

"We should get a divorce. You know, put the past behind us."

Katharine sagged against the counter, then forced herself to stand ramrod stiff. She should have expected this, should have thought of it first. Of course, a divorce made sense. They should put seven bizarre years behind them. Yet a huge knot twisted savagely in her stomach.

"Okay." She forced the word from airless lungs.

Mitch lifted a brown envelope from his lap and offered it to her. His expression cool, his eyes devoid of life, he said, "I've prepared a settlement. We'll waive the prenuptial agreement, and you'll receive a much larger cash settlement to compensate you for all you've done for me."

"No," she croaked.

"You'll never have to worry about money again, Katharine."

"I don't want your money. I never did, and you know that! How dare you salve your conscience with cash! How dare you offer me a payoff now that you no longer need anything from me!"

The stricken look on his face convinced her she'd hit home.

"No, Kat," he insisted quietly. "I want you to be free—"

She cut off his protest. "You haven't changed, have you? You decided what's best for me and set up a plan, right down to a written agreement that you expected me to sign without question. You never even asked what *I* wanted, what *I* needed!"

"But I—"

"Well, fortunately, I want a divorce. I *need* a divorce! I'll *go get* a divorce. But I don't want anything else from you. Keep every lousy penny of your money!"

She grabbed the paint can and rushed upstairs, hardly caring that paint sloshed down her leg, leaving a trail of mauve splatters on the faded carpet.

KATHARINE SAT AT HER desk at the plant, searching for ways to squeeze more money from the company's shrinking balance sheet, when the phone rang.

"Katharine, are you sitting down?" Art Harris asked, a hint of excitement in his tone.

"Art?" she asked, cautiously hopeful. She held her breath and felt her pulse jump.

"I have an offer for you."

"An *offer*? Not just an inquiry?"

"A great offer! It's from a company I wasn't familiar with, Omega-Alpha."

Relief flooded through her. "How did it happen? I didn't even meet with them."

"I got a preliminary call from them, very tentative. I checked them out and they're strong in terms of money and know-how."

"Good." She sighed.

"You've been disappointed so many times, I decided to send them your financial projections and portions of your earlier presentations. When they asked for a meeting, I suggested they talk with me first."

"And they made an *offer?*"

"They want to buy one-third of The KD Line at your price. They'll be available for advice. You'll run the company, though. I'll see you in an hour, and we'll go over the details."

Katharine replaced the receiver. Tears rolled down her cheeks, releasing a year's worth of stress. She turned her back to the office door and indulged in a cleansing cry.

A few minutes later she jumped to her feet, swabbed at her face with a tissue, and ran out on the plant floor.

"Gus!" She flung herself in his arms, nearly knocking her grandfather down. "Gus! We've got an offer! Art thinks it's a good one. We can pay off the bank and start producing the playground equipment!"

As he hugged her, Gus exclaimed, "Honey, I knew you could do it!"

KATHARINE MET WITH HER lawyer that afternoon. He agreed the offer was favorable. Astounded that he suggested no changes, Katharine signed the agreement, feeling rather smug about the deal she'd made. Maybe this offer had dropped into her lap, but she'd knocked herself out on an eight-month hunt before she found the prize. This agreement was worth every bit of the struggle.

While she was in her lawyer's office she might as well handle another problem, she decided. She asked Mark to prepare a resignation from her position as vice president of Woods, Inc. She'd cut her only tie to Mitch's business before he asked her to.

As she waited for him to return with the form, Katharine reveled in her good fortune. Without Omega-Alpha she'd had two choices: close the company and bankrupt Gus, or ask Mitch for money. Now she was free of money worries.

And Art vouched for Omega-Alpha. She recalled the few words of Greek that she'd learned as a sorority pledge. The name sounded backward since it could mean "end to beginning." Maybe the words were reversed to catch attention.

Katharine shook her head. An investment company saved The KD Line, and she worried about its name. She had no time for silly speculation. She had to get home and dress for a party. She'd treat Gus to the best meal of his life!

USING THE HARD-WON strength in his arms, Mitch moved from his new bed to the wheelchair. At last even his legs were responding to therapy. Soon he'd be able to live on his own. Then he could get out of Katharine's life.

A knock at his door startled him. When he called, "Come in," Katharine opened the sliding doors. She looked radiant, he thought, relaxed and happy. She looked the way he wanted to remember her.

"I have some news," she said, her tone more solemn than he expected. "An investor bought one-third of my company yesterday. I can start production on the Habitat, the playground equipment."

"Congratulations, Katharine," he said, his tone carefully neutral. "We should commemorate this occasion. I'll buy you dinner."

"Thank you, but Gus and I celebrated last night."

His plan was working, he thought. She'd closed him out of her life, just as he knew she must. He felt cold, numb.

"I wasn't looking for a free meal," she added tartly. "I wanted you to know that I *really* don't need your charity."

He refused to discuss his money again. "I've been thinking, Katharine . . . I should move out."

She arched a brow. "Can you?" she asked without inflection.

"I make you uncomfortable in your own house."

"Where will you go?" She seemed more curious than caring.

"To Houston. There are rehab centers and therapists there, you know."

"You don't have to move. All your equipment is here. You work well with Steve."

Her face and voice gave him no hint of her feelings. Yet her hands shook, and she grasped the back of a chair. "You're not in my way. You may as well stay here. It won't be much longer, will it?"

His heart lurched in his chest. She hadn't denied her discomfort, yet she considered his needs first. "No. A few more weeks, I think."

"Fine. Then stay." She left, closing the doors behind her.

He should congratulate himself, he thought. He'd gotten everything he wanted. He'd rebuilt his body somewhat, so Katharine would no longer feel guilty about his limitations. She'd agreed to a divorce, and now her money problems were eased.

He'd accomplished all his objectives, and he felt miserable.

WHEN THE DOORBELL CHIMED on Sunday afternoon, Mitch opened the door and found Francine smiling expectantly.

"Mitch! You're all better!" She set a large fruit basket in his lap. "I brought a little gift for my favorite invalid."

"Terrific." He eyed the selection of citrus. "We're always fighting scurvy around here. You've given us new hope."

"I'm so glad to help," Francine blathered.

He saw Katharine enter the back hall, start for the stairs, pause as if reconsidering, then walk into the foyer.

"Hello, Francine," she said with little inflection. "I didn't expect you."

"I saw no reason to call. After all, where else could Mitch be? He's crippled."

When Katharine made no reply, Mitch offered, "You'd be surprised at where I've been and what I've done."

Katharine lifted the basket from Mitch's lap without meeting his gaze. "I'll take this to the kitchen."

"Come along, Mitch. We must talk." Francine led the way into his room and closed the doors.

"Whatever is the matter with Katharine, dear? She was even less sociable than usual."

"Perhaps because she won't be related to you much longer. She's getting a divorce."

"You paid her off?"

Mitch clenched his teeth until he could speak calmly. "I convinced her it was time to end the marriage. But she refused my money—and I offered her plenty."

"How lovely! You got off scot-free."

"Hell, Francine, that was never my intention! Besides, Katharine isn't interested in my money. She's been the only person in my life who understood me."

Francine sighed. "*I* understand that you're naive. She's a manipulator. She was when you married her, and she is now."

Mitch gave up. Trying to reason with Francine was a futile exercise.

LATER ON FRANCINE WENT upstairs and interrupted Katharine as she repaired plaster in one of the bedrooms.

"My, my, dear, you've made so much progress on your restoration. Of course, with servants, I'm sure you have lots more free time."

Katharine spoke through gritted teeth. "Francine, I put in long hours at my company, time and effort that is paying off. I'm expanding the business. In addition, I keep the household on an even keel, and I try to help your brother beat his illness. I don't have free time."

"Oh, dear, don't be angry. I really must talk to you."

"Fine." Katharine led the way to the kitchen and started a pot of coffee. "What do you want?" she asked pointedly.

"Dear, Mitch is so much better now. And he said you'd finally agreed to a divorce."

"Uh-hmm," Katharine confirmed, wondering where Francine was heading.

"It's time for Mitch to begin his life all over again. He really should return to Houston."

"Really?" Francine had never understood Mitch's illness, or the difficulties of his recovery, Katharine reflected. Perhaps it was time she did.

"He can't walk, Francine. He'll need therapy for some time—no one knows how long. Someone will have to help him, make sure everything runs smoothly."

Her gaze bore into Francine's. "Do you want that job?"

Francine flushed. "I'll hire people to look after him. He'll be well taken care of. Why are you so determined to keep him here?"

"I want what's best for Mitch. It's that simple."

Francine's brow wrinkled. "That's all?"

"Yes, Francine. We're getting a divorce, but I'm not getting a cent."

"You needn't be coy, dear. I know he's taken care of you. Mitch was always generous where you were concerned."

It was all Katharine could do to contain the shriek forming in her chest. She'd put up with Francine's condescension for too many years, trying to keep peace in the family. Now it no longer mattered. She and Mitch were only a formality away from divorce.

"Katharine, you said you've recently *expanded*?"

"That's what I said. And my new line will secure my future. I built this company from the ground up, alone. I've designed an exciting new product line, and my investment consultant has found me a most enthusiastic investor, Omega-Alpha Corporation."

"Oh? And who owns this Omega-Alpha?"

"I—I'm not sure. My consultant handled the details, but he investigated them thoroughly. That's his job. That's why I hired him."

"Has it ever occurred to you that Mitch might own Omega-Alpha?"

Katharine slapped her hands over her mouth, but too late to throttle her shocked gasp. Slowly she lowered her hands to her lap, never shifting her gaze from Francine's. "What . . . ? How . . . ? Why do you think that?"

"I know my brother, Katharine. I'll wager a thousand dollars that he's Omega-Alpha. I think he finally finished what he came to Dallas to do in August—invest in your company."

HARDLY ABLE TO BREATHE, Katharine felt as if she'd been punched in the stomach. But her rapidly building rage renewed her strength. "We'll see about that!"

Francine backed toward the kitchen door. "Oh, my. I really must rush to the airport. Call me a cab, dear."

"Call your own cab! I've got more important things to do!"

Leaving Francine gaping in the kitchen, Katharine gritted her teeth, marched to Mitch's door, and pounded it with her fist. "Mitch!"

"Come in. I've got a surprise for you."

Shoving the doors apart, Katharine stomped into the room. "I've had enough of your surprises! I don't want any more of them!"

Mitch paled. "What?"

His crestfallen face left her unaffected. "Francine had a little talk with me. She bet me a thousand dollars that you own Omega-Alpha, that *you* are my new investor."

"What?" The color drained from his face.

"You heard me, Mitch. Are you Mr. Omega-Alpha?"

"Ah, Kat, let me explain," he began, gripping the arms of the wheelchair so hard his knuckles turned white.

"Explain what? You planned this months ago. Tricking me was your only reason for coming to Dallas. If you hadn't been intent on stabbing me in the back, you'd have gotten sick in Houston. Then you'd have been someone else's problem."

She saw him flinch at her cruel words, but he'd earned every one of them. "I never wanted anything from you. But you went behind my back and bought part of my company. *My* company, Mitch! I started it. I built it."

"But you needed an investor." He spoke softly, his tone defensive.

"That was my problem. I didn't want you to interfere."

"Our contract says you can buy my third at appraised value in five years."

Five years sounded like a prison sentence. "I don't want to wait that long."

"Then I'll waive it. You can buy me out at any time."

"You know I don't have the money."

"Hell, let's cancel the contract, and you can keep the damned money."

"Ah, how magnanimous of you! No, thank you! I'll pay you back as fast as I can. Right now I just want to be rid of you."

Anger flashed in his eyes. "I wanted to help you, Katharine. I wanted you to be free. You're letting pride override your business sense."

"And you have five days to clear out of my house. Out of my life! I'm going out of town on business. When I get back, I want no trace of you here."

She glared at him, hoping this was the last time she'd see him, and stalked out of her dining room.

AT NINE THE NEXT MORNING she sat stiffly in her lawyer's office. "I've decided to get a long-overdue divorce, Mark. It'll be very simple. We just don't want to be married any longer."

"Have you agreed on division of the community estate?" When she quirked a brow, he explained. "Have you agreed on how to divide what you've both accumulated over the past seven years?"

"We won't divide anything. We'll each keep what we've got."

"Are you sure? You may be entitled to a large settlement."

"I signed a prenuptial agreement. I wouldn't be entitled to much."

"Some of those agreements are invalid. We might be able to set it aside. I understand Mr. Woods is rather wealthy."

Katharine hated this venal discussion. "I know you're looking after my interests, Mark, but I don't want anything from the man, except a divorce."

"Has he agreed to it?"

"He suggested it," she said sharply.

"I see. Then perhaps he'll sign a waiver so he won't have to show up in court."

"I want this to be over as quickly as possible."

"I'll courier over the divorce petition and waiver today. He can contact his lawyer if he wishes. I'll file the case as soon as I can, Katharine."

She stood numbly as Mark rounded his desk and took her arm. His calm voice offered reassurance. "Sixty days after that, you and I will go to court, I'll ask you ten questions, and it will be over."

Unsteady on her feet, Katharine kept a hand on the wall as Mark closed the door behind her. Sixty days, she thought, dismayed. Sixty days of "My lawyer will call your lawyer." Even then, it was far from finished. It would only be over when she repaid Mitch every cent, with interest.

SPRING SUN DAPPLED the open courtyard of one of New Orleans's fine old restaurants. Dixieland jazz drifted toward Katharine as she contemplated her host, Charles Broussard.

"Remember the first time I brought you here to The Court of the Two Sisters, Miss Katharine?"

His use of "Miss" always made her feel as though she were standing on a pedestal, swathed in crinolines and petticoats. Only dear old Mr. Broussard would call her that while treating her as a business colleague.

"I remember it well. You called my office about two years ago and demanded to buy my furniture—sight unseen."

"Oh, I hadn't seen it, but Marie saw it at a friend's house in Dallas. Can you imagine how it broke this old man's heart when my daughter said she wanted The KD Line for my grandbaby? None of my furniture was good enough!"

Katharine smiled. "You were my first big customer, Mr. Broussard. When I got orders from all your stores, I started believing I could succeed. I've always been grateful."

"No point in being grateful, Miss Katharine. You do good work, and you've got a good head on your shoulders. You were bound to be discovered. And, of course, introducing your line in this area gave me a jump on the competition."

He rubbed his hands together, obviously enjoying his coup. "Now, about this playground equipment. Have you sold to any of my competitors in Baton Rouge, New Orleans or Lafayette?"

When she shook her head, he continued, "I've never carried outdoor products, but this is mighty attractive. I'd like to order plenty for my stores. I'll display the biggest pieces on the parking lots to get customers' attention."

His eyes twinkling, he added, "And old Charles will trounce his competitors."

Katharine gulped. She'd decided to begin production on the Habitat even though she'd been coerced into using Mitch's money. She was responsible to her grandfather and the bank; she couldn't quit.

All week long during her business trip, customers were impressed with the Habitat and she'd made several sales; but once again, Mr. Broussard's huge order would establish the line.

Katharine savored her iced tea. She'd have to sell a heck of a lot of playground pieces in order to pay off Mitch, but she'd gotten a start today.

Mr. Broussard interrupted her reverie. "Miss Katharine, I know starting up a line is expensive, and I've got faith in you. If you ever need money, I'd like to have first shot at buying a stake in your company."

Katharine clutched her glass in surprise. "What?"

"I didn't mean to offend you, Miss Katharine, implying that you needed money. But I'm always looking for good investments."

If only she'd known that a week ago! Charles Broussard would be a fair and honorable partner. If only she'd found him before Mitch had "saved" her company. Then hope surged through her when she remembered Mitch's offer.

"I recently sold a third of the company to another investor, but it isn't working very well."

"What would it take for me to buy him out?"

Katharine named the enormous sum, expecting the old man to blanch.

"Miss Katharine, I'll assume that other gentleman's contract."

Afraid to believe in her good fortune, Katharine tried to give her mentor an out. "You haven't reviewed the contract or my books—"

"I know the quality of your furniture, and I know my customers buy it like crazy. In four or five years, Miss Katharine, you'll be making lots of money, and then I'll expect to get my share."

KATHARINE SAT ON THE edge of the bed in her hotel room. In a few days she'd settle up with Mitch. She'd sign her name to a few documents and cut the last ties that bound her to him. There'd be only the formality of the sixty days' wait until she would be legally free.

She ought to celebrate and order a bottle of champagne, call a few friends. But who would she call? She hadn't worried Gus with the truth about Omega-Alpha, so she couldn't call him.

She ought to call Mitch, she thought sourly, and gloat. But she wanted to see his face when she announced her buyout.

She wandered restlessly around the small room, trying to work up enthusiasm for champagne. Suddenly she picked up the phone and ordered a huge box of Swiss chocolates instead. Chocolate—her favorite comfort food.

When the candy arrived, Katharine settled into a warm bath and nibbled sweets until the water turned cold.

Climbing into bed, she was very pleased with herself. She'd have peace for the first time since September, when Mitch had reentered her life. In the past seven months, everything had changed—she sighed and nestled into her pillow—and nothing had changed. She'd fallen for the same wrong man a second time. She marveled at her stupidity.

She'd fallen for the same Mitch who made her dependent on him, made her decisions for her. The same Mitch who only found her convenient for a while; who insisted on dominating her.

She'd known all along that he didn't love her. Yet, when he made love to her with such passion and tenderness, she'd let herself hope that he did.

She rolled on her back and cupped her head with her hands. A tiny voice in her mind accused her of being unfair. True, Mitch hadn't chased her around his bed, she admitted. She'd been as aggressive as he. She flushed, recalling her performance in the green dress.

But he'd kept making decisions for her, she reminded herself, determined to remain angry. He'd bought that security system without telling her. And she—*they* had needed security in that old house, the nagging voice noted. He lied to her about the Wysocki deal. But, of course, she'd neglected to mention that she had a meeting to prepare for.

Try as she might, Katharine failed to find evidence of domination. Most people would think the security system was a generous gift, intended to make her . . . safe. Perhaps Mitch was only worried about his own safety. Perhaps he cared for her in his own way. Perhaps he felt guilty for using her.

He'd offered her money with no strings attached, he'd claimed, and she'd been offended. But she had blamed *him* for not helping her financially years ago.

Still, he'd bought into her company; and she despised his betrayal. After she'd explicitly told him not to interfere in her financial matters, he had—secretly.

Katharine punched her pillow. For at least seven months he'd planned to buy into her company. Why had he waited so long? He'd known from the beginning how badly she needed an investor. Did he give her time to find help on her own and step in only when she was on the brink of failure, or had he enjoyed watching her struggle and fail?

The agreement he offered clearly left her in charge of the company. She owned two-thirds of the stock, so she could do anything she wanted without his approval. Her lawyer had pointed out that she could even sell her shares to someone else if she decided to. What did Mitch expect to get from the deal, or from her?

He'd said, "I want you to be free." Free? Was the investment his idea of a payoff, as she'd believed? Cash for her time and attention—and love? Or did he want to make her secure against financial worries?

Katharine sprang out of bed and paced, struggling to be rational about the thoughts and emotions agitating her. Admittedly—though she had gone out of her way not to admit it to herself—her relationship with him was very complicated.

Sure, he gave her gifts; but lots of women wanted their men to indulge them. Besides, the place mats and doorbell were hardly extravagances. For the first time, he'd made a gift for her and considered her needs. Perhaps he'd wanted to show he cared for her.

Katharine, I don't want your pity. She recalled his stammered words, his closed expression, and shuddered. Living with GBS required him to make adjustments that the healthy Mitch had never contemplated. The trip to San Francisco and the Wine Country had drained him physically and mentally. Perhaps he believed he was worthy only of pity, yet she doubted that she'd have had the courage that Mitch had displayed from the day he fell ill.

Maybe she'd been unfair. She'd acted overly suspicious and unreasonably stubborn at times, always jumping to the conclusion that he was the same old Mitch.

She should apologize to Mitch for her culpability. She must at least make peace with him—otherwise she'd never be at peace with herself.

In a few hours her flight left for Dallas. She wished she were there now. She tried to relax, but so many questions, fears and uncertainties jostled for her attention.

She'd see him tomorrow.

Then she remembered: Mitch was gone.

She was too late.

KATHARINE UNLOCKED the front door of her house, stepped into the foyer, and entered her security code into the keypad on the wall. She stroked the small plastic box that had stirred such resentment in her. Even though Mitch was gone, he'd left memories that would make it hard to forget him.

She thought about phoning him, but knew they needed to talk face-to-face. Weary from her emotional turmoil, she considered a flight to Houston.

"Katharine?"

Mitch! She opened the doors to the dining room. He sat in his wheelchair, watching her warily.

"I haven't left yet. . . ."

"It's all right." She struggled to still her shaking hands and marshal her thoughts. "I'd like to talk with you."

She sat in the secretary's chair so she and Mitch would be eye to eye. She drew a deep breath. "I found another investor," she said tentatively. "I can pay you back."

Tension lines deepened around his eyes and mouth. "I see. You got what you wanted, then?"

"I thought so at first, but . . ."

"But?" He held her gaze and she saw something flare in his eyes. Hope?

Encouraged a little, she continued. "Accepting your money was only one part of my problem. I assumed that you wanted to run my life as you did before, so I overreacted when you made decisions for me. I'm sorry I was so suspicious of you."

She paused to gain strength and banish the uncertainty from her tone. "I'm sorry I said 'I love you' and put you on the spot. I probably have other things to apologize for, but I don't understand everything yet."

"Do you love me now, Katharine?"

She hated him at that instant. How dare he embarrass her as she struggled to right old wrongs!

She stiffened, determined to speak the truth even if he hurt her again. "Yes! But you know that. I told you!" she blurted. "And I've never pitied you. Why should I? You have almost everything a man could want!"

"I finally figured that out." A smile played on his lips.

"How?"

Mitch chuckled. "When you yelled at me and ordered me out of your house. A soft touch like you would never unleash such fury on someone you pitied. You'd have buried your frustrations and coped.

"I should have realized that long ago," he added. "When I rejected your love, you should have been relieved. But you weren't."

Katharine held her breath, waiting for his next words, hoping against hope.

"Come to the backyard with me."

She repeated blankly, "The backyard?"

Still clutching her briefcase, Katharine followed Mitch as he rolled through the house and down the ramp. She watched the play of muscles and sinews in his arms and back. He was so strong now, she realized.

And then she looked up. Her drab yard with its few scraggly shrubs was gone, replaced by a Victorian flower garden. Too awed to speak, she sat on an iron bench beneath the oak tree and reveled in the beauty Mitch had created for her. Row upon row of riotous blossoms—slashes of pink, purple, gold and white—filled her yard. In the spring air wafted the heavy sweetness of roses, honeysuckle and wisteria. In the center of the emerald lawn stood a fountain, its splashing water falling into a fish pond. Katharine felt slightly dizzy trying to absorb all the beauty at once.

"I hope you don't mind that I did this. But when you left and I got the divorce papers, I knew I had to act fast if there was any chance . . ."

He cleared his throat. "So I'm courting you with flowers and perfume, just like you wanted."

"I could never have imagined this. It's so lovely."

"I guess I went a little overboard, but I had a lot to make up for."

Teary eyed, she sat there, dumbfounded.

His voice husky, he continued. "I came to Dallas to invest in your company. Then I was going to get a divorce, and give the stock back to you, so you'd always know you owed your success to me. I'd felt hurt and abandoned for three years. I was so confused that I wanted to help you and hurt you at the same time.

"I told myself I no longer needed you or loved you. Then you came to see me at the hospital, and you stayed, and *cared*. And I knew I'd lied to myself. But I had nothing to offer you, except uncertainty."

"That never mattered to me," she whispered hoarsely.

"But it mattered to me, Kat. You'd made yourself so strong, so independent. I couldn't tie you to me because you felt sorry for me. The best I could do was see to it that you'd have your freedom—to make you financially secure and free of any obligations you thought you owed me."

"Ending the past. Beginning the future."

"Yes. Omega-Alpha."

Katharine clenched her fists in her lap. "I had no idea . . ." she said.

"I realize that now. But I acted like a businessman and looked for a simple, logical, monetary solution. Besides," he chided, "*you* left, and you never even hinted that we could be anything more than friends—and occasional lovers."

"Because I believed you didn't love me, didn't need me, except until you got well." She paused to draw strength. "Even if you loved me, I knew I couldn't go back to our old relationship. I saw no future. Only the present—and the past."

"We nearly let the past destroy us again." Mitch took her hand, nestling it between his palms. "I love you, Katharine. I want us to be together."

I love you, Katharine. The words she'd so wanted to hear. But she tamped her joy, knowing their differences. "I want us to be together, too, Mitch. But can we? We must trust each other."

"We're finally starting to learn."

"We didn't live together very well."

"We've been together here for six months, and it's been wonderful, except for the occasional explosion when I got out of line or you overreacted."

"Sometimes it was wonderful." She shoved aside the warm memories that crowded into her mind. "But it's been an artificial situation, not real life. In real life, I can't go back to Houston—to our old life. I'm not the kind of wife you want, or need. I never gave you the support or encouragement a man should expect."

"You're not the kind of wife I *used* to want. But you've grown and changed. You encouraged me when I was ready to give up. You've become exactly the woman I should have wanted all along. It just took me a while to understand that."

His hands tightened around hers. "I've changed, too, Katharine. Haven't I?"

"I think so." A smile played at the corners of her mouth. "All for the better, too."

He surveyed the garden. "I thought we'd live here."

"Here? At my house?"

"I'd like us to be a family, Kat. The kind of family you have—warm, caring, sharing each other's joys and woes. I want to start filling some of those bedrooms with kids. We can get them ready-made if you want to, but you're such a dedicated do-it-yourselfer, I figured . . ." He winked.

"Oh, Mitch, are you sure?" she asked, desperate for his confirmation.

His expression grew serious. "I've never been more sure of anything. I want us to start our lives over, together."

"You'd choose to live here?"

"I want to live wherever you are. I've proved I can run my company from Dallas, leaving the day-to-day details to Sam. You and Gus can continue operating your company."

He hesitated for a moment, then added in a neutral tone, "You have your investor, so you won't need my money if it bothers you." He lowered his voice to a throaty whisper. "But the other guy will want to make money. If I'm your 'investor,' I won't care about profits. You can give away as much playground equipment as you want."

"Still the master of seduction, aren't you?"

Mitch laughed—a hearty, happy sound that rumbled from his chest.

She rose and hurried across the patio toward her briefcase. As she removed some papers, he called, "Don't turn around yet."

Curious, Katharine heard strange scraping sounds.

"Okay," he said.

She pivoted. Mitch stood upright, leaning on crutches, grinning.

"Mitch! When . . ."

"I walked the day you found out about Omega-Alpha. This was the surprise I wanted to show you before you ordered me out. I hid the crutches behind some flowers today, hoping . . ."

Overjoyed, she stepped toward him.

"No. Stay there."

Her heart swelling with emotion, Katharine watched Mitch as he walked haltingly across the new, smooth patio until he stood before her.

Tears glistening in her eyes, she folded the divorce petition into an unwieldy paper airplane and lofted it. She laughed when it crashed into the fountain, then sank in the fish pond.

"Great shot, Kat."

She wrapped her arms around his waist. "I love you, Mitch. I always will. I want to be with you."

Caught in her loving embrace, he spoke softly, "I, Mitchell, take you, Katharine, to be my wife—"

Katharine inserted quickly, "*Forever*, this time."

HARLEQUIN Temptation

Rebels & Rogues

Brew: He'd fought his way off the streets . . . but his past threatened the woman he loved.

THE BAD BOY
by Roseanne Williams
Temptation #401, July 1992

All men are not created equal. Some are rough around the edges. Tough-minded but tenderhearted. Incredibly sexy. The tempting fulfillment of every woman's fantasy.

When it's time to fight for what they believe in, to win that special woman, our Rebels and Rogues are heroes at heart. Twelve Rebels and Rogues, one each month in 1992, only from Harlequin Temptation. Don't miss the upcoming books by our fabulous authors such as JoAnn Ross, Ruth Jean Dale and Janice Kaiser.

OVER THE YEARS, TELEVISION HAS BROUGHT
THE LIVES AND LOVES OF MANY CHARACTERS INTO
YOUR HOMES. NOW HARLEQUIN INTRODUCES YOU
TO THE TOWN AND PEOPLE OF

One small town—twelve terrific love stories.

GREAT READING...GREAT SAVINGS...
AND A FABULOUS FREE GIFT!

Each book set in Tyler is a self-contained love story; together, the
twelve novels stitch the fabric of the community.

By collecting proofs-of-purchase found in each Tyler book, you can
receive a fabulous gift, ABSOLUTELY FREE! And use our special
Tyler coupons to save on your next TYLER book purchase.

Join us for the fifth TYLER book,
BLAZING STAR by Suzanne Ellison, available in July.

Is there really a murder cover-up?
Will Brick and Karen overcome differences and find true love?

FREE GIFT OFFER

To receive your free gift, send us the specified number of proofs-of-purchase from any specially marked Free Gift Offer Harlequin or Silhouette book with the Free Gift Certificate properly completed, plus a check or money order (do not send cash) to cover postage and handling payable to Harlequin/Silhouette Free Gift Promotion Offer. We will send you the specified gift.

FREE GIFT CERTIFICATE

ITEM	A. GOLD TONE EARRINGS	B. GOLD TONE BRACELET	C. GOLD TONE NECKLACE
# of proofs-of-purchase required	3	6	9
Postage and Handling	$1.75	$2.25	$2.75
Check one	☐	☐	☐

Name: _____

Address: _____

City: _____ State: _____ Zip Code: _____

Mail this certificate, specified number of proofs-of-purchase and a check or money order for postage and handling to: HARLEQUIN/SILHOUETTE FREE GIFT OFFER 1992, P.O. Box 9057, Buffalo, NY 14269-9057. Requests must be received by July 31, 1992.

PLUS—Every time you submit a completed certificate with the correct number of proofs-of-purchase, you are automatically entered in our MILLION DOLLAR SWEEPSTAKES! No purchase or obligation necessary to enter. See below for alternate means of entry and how to obtain complete sweepstakes rules.

MILLION DOLLAR SWEEPSTAKES
NO PURCHASE OR OBLIGATION NECESSARY TO ENTER

To enter, hand-print (mechanical reproductions are not acceptable) your name and address on a 3"×5" card and mail to Million Dollar Sweepstakes 6097, c/o either P.O. Box 9056, Buffalo, NY 14269-9056 or P.O. Box 621, Fort Erie, Ontario L2A 5X3. Limit: one entry per envelope. Entries must be sent via 1st-class mail. For eligibility, entries must be received no later than March 31, 1994. No liability is assumed for printing errors, lost, late or misdirected entries.

Sweepstakes is open to persons 18 years of age or older. All applicable laws and regulations apply. Sweepstakes offer void wherever prohibited by law. Prizewinners will be determined no later than May 1994. Chances of winning are determined by the number of entries distributed and received. For a copy of the Official Rules governing this sweepstakes offer, send a self-addressed, stamped envelope (WA residents need not affix return postage) to Million Dollar Sweepstakes Rules, P.O. Box 4733, Blair, NE 68009.

HT3U

ONE PROOF-OF-PURCHASE

To collect your fabulous FREE GIFT you must include the necessary FREE GIFT proofs-of-purchase with a properly completed offer certificate.

(See inside back cover for offer details)